VAIBHAV KUMAR

PRABHAT
PRAKASHAN

Published by
PRABHAT PRAKASHAN PVT. LTD.
4/19 Asaf Ali Road,
New Delhi-110 002 (INDIA)
e-mail: prabhatbooks@gmail.com

ISBN 978-93-5562-349-2

VIKRAM SARABHAI: A COMPLETE BIOGRAPHY
by Vaibhav Kumar

Edition
First, 2024

Price
₹ 400 (Rupees Four Hundred Only)

Printed at
Sanjay Printers, Sahibabad

Author's Note

In the rich tapestry of modern Indian history, Vikram Sarabhai shines as an inspirational personality who helped transform India into a technologically progressive nation. As the father of India's Space Program and the pioneer behind several prestigious institutions, his vision and contributions still reverberate today.

This book aims to chronicle Sarabhai's renowned yet lesser known journey - from his formative years as the scion of the illustrious Sarabhai family, to his academic pursuits at Cambridge and cosmic ray research with Nobel Laureate C.F. Powell that cemented his passion for science. It will spotlight his steadfast leadership in establishing the Indian Space Research Organisation (ISRO) and the Physical Research Laboratory (PRL), which catalysed space research and nuclear power development in India.

Beyond science, Sarabhai was a progressive institution builder - founding institutions ranging from the Nehru Foundation to the Indian Institute of Management to propel India's growth story. As a pioneering entrepreneur, his statistics venture laid the foundation for India's market research industry. On the cultural front, along with his wife Mrinalini, a celebrated classical dancer herself, he helped resuscitate India's arts.

It captures the multifaceted legacy of this remarkable polymath while highlighting little known facets of his life - from his student days in Cambridge to his affection for the arts to his guiding philosophy of science for social good that still powers India's space odyssey. It will feature reminisces from the people he closely inspired, including scientists and family members.

❑

Contents

Introduction

In the books of Indian history, few names shine as brightly as that of Vikram Ambalal Sarabhai Jain. Born into the esteemed Sarabhai family on 12 August 1919, Vikram Sarabhai emerged as a pivotal figure in the realms of physics and astronomy. His unparalleled dedication led to the inception of space research in India and significantly contributed to the country's nuclear power development.

A recipient of the prestigious Padma Bhushan in 1966 and posthumously awarded the Padma Vibhushan in 1972, Sarabhai's legacy transcended the boundaries of science. The son of Ambalal Sarabhai, he was deeply rooted in a family renowned for its industrial prowess and unwavering commitment to India's independence movement. In 1942, Vikram Sarabhai married Mrinalini, a distinguished classical dancer, and together they raised two children, Mallika and Kartikeya, who both carved their paths in activism and science, respectively.

Sarabhai's journey in academia took him from Gujarat College, Ahmedabad, to the prestigious University of Cambridge, England. There, he completed his tripos in natural sciences in 1940, later returning to pursue a PhD with his thesis 'Cosmic Ray Investigations in Tropical Latitudes' in 1947. That same year marked the founding of the Physical Research Laboratory (PRL) in Ahmedabad, an institution that would become synonymous with space sciences in India. Starting humbly at his residence,

'The Retreat', the institute initially focused on cosmic ray research before expanding its horizons.

Under Sarabhai's visionary leadership, PRL was formally established at the MG Science Institute, Ahmedabad, with support from various educational foundations. The institute, initially led by Kalpathi Ramakrishna Ramanathan, broadened its research scope to encompass theoretical physics and radio physics, aided by grants from the Atomic Energy Commission.

But Sarabhai's interests were not confined to science alone. He was a man of diverse passions, ranging from sports to statistics. He founded the Operations Research Group (ORG), India's first market research organisation, and was instrumental in establishing several key institutions, including the Nehru Foundation for Development, the Indian Institute of Management Ahmedabad (IIM-A), and the Darpana Academy of Performing Arts, co-founded with his wife.

Sarabhai's contributions extended to numerous projects, such as the Fast Breeder Test Reactor in Kalpakkam and the Indian Space Research Organisation, culminating in the launch of India's first satellite, Aryabhata, in 1975. Tragically, on 30 December 1971, just hours after a conversation with APJ Abdul Kalam, Vikram Sarabhai passed away due to cardiac arrest, leaving behind a legacy that continues to inspire generations.

With this book, we are about to witness the journey of one of the greatest minds born on Indian soil. Let's begin.

❑

Background: Before Vikram Sarabhai

Ahmedabad, a vibrant and dynamic city, is often regarded as the quintessential heart of India, encapsulating the country's rich and diverse cultural tapestry. As you step into this bustling metropolis, you're immediately enveloped by its warm and welcoming atmosphere, a testament to the city's inherent spirit of inclusivity and hospitality. Ahmedabad isn't just a destination; it's a journey into the soul of India, offering a vivid portrayal of what it truly means to experience this magnificent country.

Renowned for its celebration of all things 'Indian', Ahmedabad is a city that effortlessly kindles a deep-seated love for India within the hearts of those who wander its streets. The city isn't merely a place; it's an emotion, an experience that stays with you long after you've left its borders. From the bustling markets to the quiet corners, every nook of Ahmedabad echoes with stories of India's glorious past and promising future.

For those seeking to delve into India's historical essence, the residential areas of Ahmedabad are a must-visit. These neighbourhoods are bastions of history, where traditional architectural styles have been meticulously preserved, serving as windows into a bygone era. Among the most notable of these are the Muslim enclave of Bhadra, renowned for its majestic mosques; the Hindu quarters of Bohra and Jhaveri, celebrated for their ornate temples and intricate architecture; and the Zoroastrian sector of Chandi Chowk, distinguished by its revered fire temple.

Each of these areas offers a unique glimpse into the diverse religious and cultural fabric of Ahmedabad, showcasing the harmonious coexistence of different communities. The architectural splendour of these neighbourhoods is not just about buildings and structures; it's a narrative of the people, their beliefs, and their way of life.

Moreover, Ahmedabad holds a special place in the annals of Indian history as the birthplace of the illustrious MrVikram Sarabhai. A visionary who played a pivotal role in shaping modern India, Sarabhai's contributions have left an indelible mark on the nation. His legacy in Ahmedabad isn't just a point of pride for the city; it's a beacon of inspiration, symbolising the city's significant role in the country's journey towards progress and innovation.

In essence, Ahmedabad is more than just a city. It's a mosaic of history, culture, architecture, and legacy, each piece telling a story of India's rich heritage and its unyielding spirit of resilience and advancement. Whether it's through its ancient streets, sacred temples, or the memory of its great sons, Ahmedabad invites you to discover the heart of India, one unforgettable experience at a time.

Gujaratis, as a whole, are renowned for their exceptional entrepreneurial spirit, setting them apart as one of the most economically astute communities across India. This distinct community is characterised by a deep-rooted ethos that seamlessly integrates traditional values with a sharp acumen for business and commerce. The primary ambition for many within this group is to devise and implement strategies that maximise financial success, marking them as a significant and influential segment in the socio-economic landscape of the country.

This entrepreneurial spirit among Gujaratis is not confined to any specific region; it's a widespread characteristic that resonates throughout the community, regardless of their geographic location. They have a long-standing history of engaging in trade and commerce, not just within the confines of India but extending to global markets. Their approach to business is marked by a profound understanding of market dynamics, adaptability to economic changes, and an innate knack for identifying and capitalising on lucrative opportunities.

This business-oriented mindset is deeply ingrained in their culture and often passed down through generations. Gujarati families emphasise the importance of education, particularly in fields related to commerce, finance, and business management. This emphasis has led to the community producing some of India's most successful entrepreneurs and business leaders, contributing substantially to the nation's economic development.

The pursuit of wealth among Gujaratis is more than a quest for personal enrichment. It's closely linked to their cultural values, which include a strong sense of community, philanthropy, and familial bonds. The wealth they accumulate is frequently channelled back into the community through various initiatives, including educational programmes, healthcare services, and other philanthropic activities. This demonstrates a holistic approach to wealth—one that encompasses both material success and community welfare.

Furthermore, the Gujarati approach to business is often characterised by innovation, foresight, and a willingness to take calculated risks. This propensity for venturing into new markets and embracing innovative business models has led to the flourishing of Gujarati enterprises in various sectors, both within India and internationally.

The Gujarati community, known for its strong entrepreneurial ethos, plays a pivotal role in the economic tapestry of India. Their focus on financial success is intricately linked to their cultural values, blending personal achievement with community development. This unique approach to business and life makes them a distinguished and vital part of India's diverse cultural and economic fabric.

Ahmedabad, historically celebrated for its prosperity and vibrant culture, has long been an integral stopover for travellers, tracing back to mythological times. It's said that even the Pandavas, figures central to the Indian epic Mahabharata, paused in this city during their legendary journeys. In addition to its mythological connections, Ahmedabad has also been a pivotal waypoint for Hajj pilgrims on their sacred journey to Makkah, further emphasising its importance as a cultural and religious hub.

The flourishing of Ahmedabad can be largely attributed to the visionary leadership of Sultan Ahmed Shah, who played a crucial role in the city's development. Recognising the potential of this region, he invited a diverse group of merchants, weavers, and craftsmen to settle there. This strategic move laid the foundation for Ahmedabad's transformation into a bustling centre of commerce and industry.

The industrious nature and thriftiness of its inhabitants turned Ahmedabad into a thriving trade hub. The city became renowned for its exquisite production of textiles and crafts. Its markets were filled with fine cotton, smooth velvet, and luxurious silver and gold brocade. The quality of these materials was so high that they were sought after not only in India but also in international markets. Indigo, a highly prized dye, was another significant export that flowed from Ahmedabad through the port of Cambay, reaching regions as far-flung as the Middle East, Europe, Africa and South Asia.

The city's strategic location and its industrious people made it an important node in international trade routes. Western imports, including a variety of goods and luxury items, were stocked in Ahmedabad's warehouses. These imports were then transported, often on the backs of donkeys and camels, to various prominent cities and royal courts across India, including Delhi, Agra, Rajasthan and Malwa.

This bustling trade not only brought economic prosperity to Ahmedabad but also fostered a rich cultural exchange. The city became a melting pot of different cultures, traditions and ideas, as traders and pilgrims from various parts of the world passed through. This blend of cultural influences is reflected in the city's architecture, cuisine and traditions, making it a unique testament to the historical and cultural richness of India.

By the mid-19th century, Ahmedabad's traditional merchants faced intense competition from Chinese and other Indian traders. This competitive pressure compelled them to explore new methods of wealth creation. In 1861, a pivotal change was initiated by Ranchodlal Chotalal, a Nagar Brahmin entrepreneur, who established the first modern steam-driven cotton mill in Ahmedabad. This venture was a daring and risky move, especially considering the historical and economic context.

Cotton was a native crop of India, and Indian spinning techniques had once been so renowned that they captivated the weavers in Blackburn and Bolton. This admiration led the East India Company to establish karkhanas (workshops) throughout Gujarat. However, this golden era had faded. Technological advancements such as the power loom, the introduction of railways, and protective tariffs in Britain had shifted the market dynamics, favouring British textile goods over Indian ones.

The timing for starting a cotton venture in Ahmedabad seemed inauspicious. The city, lacking a nearby port and plagued by a dry climate, was not an ideal location for cotton textile manufacturing. Despite these challenges, Ranchodlal Chotalal, embodying the tenacious spirit of an Ahmedabadi, was resolute in his ambition to establish a textile mill. His journey to realise this ambition was fraught with difficulties; the initial shipment of machinery was lost at sea, and the first technician he employed succumbed to cholera. Nonetheless, overcoming these hurdles, he successfully founded the Ahmedabad Spinning and Weaving Company in 1861. This enterprise was a joint stock company, with one of its shareholders being Maganbhai Karamchand, the son of Karamchand Premchand. This bold step by Ranchodlal not only marked a significant shift in Ahmedabad's industrial landscape but also represented a defiant stand against the odds, driven by a vision to revive and modernise India's textile industry.

Maganbhai was unquestionably a charismatic individual, and his extravagant character was the subject of numerous anecdotes. Stories of his substantial wealth circulated widely. As he travelled in his palki (palanquin), he made it rain coins on the streets behind him, symbolising his affluence.

In 1877, a major fire engulfed Sarangpur and Zaveri Vad, and in its aftermath, a surprising discovery was made. Jewels were found embedded in the shattered pieces of the wall from his residence, serving as evidence of the immense riches that Maganbhai possessed.

However, Maganbhai was not just a lavish spender; he also directed a portion of his riches toward public welfare. He established a Jain pathshala (religious school) and Jain temples, demonstrating his devotion to his faith. Moreover, he made a substantial contribution to education by donating funds to establish Ahmedabad's first girls' school, which was named the Maganbhai Karamchand Girls' School. Interestingly, this philanthropic act had an element of foresight to it, as it was for his own Vaishnavite daughter-in-law, Godavariba. She was renowned for her avid reading habits and was rumoured to keep a copy of Shakespeare's Hamlet under her pillow, highlighting her intellectual pursuits.

Despite his involvement in the pioneering textile company, Maganbhai and other members of the Jain community were hesitant to directly enter the textile business. Their reluctance stemmed from a fear of social exclusion within their community. A prior incident in 1878, when a Visa Porwad Jain had established a mill, had led to protests within the community. The primary concern was that insects could potentially infest the raw cotton as it passed through the machines, leading to these reservations about embracing the new industry.

As time passed, commercial interests gradually gained prominence over religious objections. By the time Sarabhai, Maganbhai's grandson and heir, reached adulthood, Ahmedabad saw the establishment of several textile mills, many of which were owned by Jains. In 1880, when the city's initial mechanised cloth printing factory, the Ahmedabad Calico Printing Company Limited, faced failure and was offered for acquisition to its largest lender, the pedhi of Karamchand Premchand, Sarabhai saw no reason to decline the opportunity. He acquired the mill and initiated its expansion, incorporating spinning and weaving into its operations. This laid the foundation for what would eventually become the family's flagship concern, Calico.

Unfortunately, Sarabhai did not live long enough to witness the fruition of his efforts. Both he and his wife passed away at a young age, leaving behind three young children: Ansuya, aged eleven, an infant named Kanta, and the boy who would grow up to be Vikram's father, the five-year-old Ambalal.

Inside the towering grey building designed by the acclaimed French architect Le Corbusier in 1954, which serves as the home of the Ahmedabad Millowners' Association (AMA), there exists a room adorned with portraits of past AMA presidents. Ambalal Sarabhai is easily distinguishable among them, as he stands alone in Western-style attire. His dark hair is neatly combed back from a broad forehead, and the round glasses covering his eyes give off an impression of either sternness or reserve—it's difficult to ascertain which.

Vikram and his father almost looked the same. It would be challenging to discern that they were father and son. This is because, aside from his fair complexion, Vikram did not inherit his father's physical traits; instead, he took after his mother with bright eyes and distinctive features. Nonetheless, the influence of the man with the inscrutable expression in his photograph would profoundly impact Vikram's life and that of his siblings.

"Ambalal was the architect of the Sarabhai legacy," asserts Kartikeya, Vikram's son. The profound contemplation that shaped Vikram's diverse personality was actually undertaken by his father, a generation prior.

Ambalal Sarabhai was an extraordinary man, particularly unconventional for his era. He possessed a deep well of knowledge and exhibited a wide range of interests, leading Erikson to aptly label him as 'a Renaissance man, Indian style'. However, Ambalal's character was extraordinarily intricate, marked by numerous contradictory facets. One of the most notable traits was his precocity.

After the untimely loss of his parents, Ambalal was raised by a paternal uncle. A portrait of him, crafted by the eminent artist of the time, Raja Ravi Varma, portrays him in a loose cloak, an embroidered cap, and a pearl necklace, with his hand gently resting on a globe. It's a strikingly pompous pose, especially for a twelve-year-old. Yet, it offers a glimpse into the lofty self-perception Ambalal held, even in his youth, as the heir to the Sarabhai fortune.

Tragedy struck when his uncle, Chimanbhai Nagindas, passed away. At the tender age of eighteen, Ambalal found himself responsible for overseeing two textile mills, Calico and Jubilee, as well as the pedhi of Karamchand Premchand, along with a substantial fortune. Additionally, he became the head of a household that included his two young sisters, a widowed aunt, and three cousins. Ambalal's journey was characterised by the weight of immense responsibilities and a unique blend of intellectual prowess and self-assuredness.

According to his grandson, Kartikeya, the early burden of responsibility compelled Ambalal to 'detach himself from the external world and introspect'. However, it's reasonable to surmise that Ambalal's contemplative disposition was also profoundly influenced by his religious beliefs. The Sarabhais were not just devout Jains; they held positions of leadership within their sect, a role that was passed down to Ambalal when he reached maturity.

Over time, Ambalal chose to step away from both his sect and the larger Jain community. Nevertheless, it is reasonable to assume that the philosophical underpinnings of Jainism continued to exert a profound impact on him. A passage from Lawrence A Babb's work, Ascetics and Kings in a Jain Ritual Culture, aptly captures the type of spiritual striving that both Ambalal and later Vikram appeared to embrace:

"A Tirthankar is one who has conquered the attachments and aversions that stand in the way of liberation from worldly bondage. By means of his own efforts and entirely without the benefit of being taught by others, he has achieved that state of omniscience in which all things are known to him—past, present, and future. But, before final attainment of his own liberation, the Tirthankar imparts his self-gained liberating knowledge to others so that they might become victors too. Thus, he establishes a crossing place for other beings."

If Ambalal's inclination to 'look within' was rooted in his religious upbringing, his intellectual ideas were shaped by exposure to Western liberal thought through his extensive reading. The result was a fascinating fusion of Eastern and Western philosophies, modernism and tradition. In her book Akhand Divo, Ambalal's daughter, Leena Mangaldas, describes her father's core values as 'self-respect', 'self-reliance', and 'self-evolution'. Ambalal's unique blend of spirituality and progressive thinking laid the foundation for the distinctive Sarabhai identity.

Ambalal was deeply aware of, and even took pride in, his philosophical inclinations. Many years later, during a conversation with Ted Standing, a British teacher employed to educate his children, Ambalal revealed his desire to break away from the demands of business, if only for a few moments, to contemplate deeper and more enduring matters. He confessed, "I would like to be able to get away from it all for a few minutes to meditate on something deeper and more permanent."

Upon unexpectedly assuming the role of the family patriarch following his uncle's passing, the young Ambalal perceived an opportunity to put some of his experimental ideas into practice. The personal sphere held the most potential, especially considering that both he and his sister Kanta were yet to marry. In both cases, Ambalal, driven by his budding idealism, chose spouses whose social status and wealth differed significantly from their own. In Kanta's case, Ambalal's decision was guided by a hopeful belief in the superiority of education over wealth. Kanta's husband was a modestly positioned mechanical engineer, and unfortunately, their marriage did not find happiness, ultimately leading to her untimely demise—an event that haunted Ambalal for the rest of his life.

These unions, characterised by disparities, caused a considerable stir within the community. Angry Jains even threatened to disrupt the wedding processions, but these threats failed to deter the determined young Ambalal. He ventured further by taking the audacious step of aiding his elder sister, Ansuya, in escaping the constraints of her child marriage. At her request, he arranged for her to embark on a journey to England, breaking with tradition and challenging societal norms in pursuit of their individual aspirations.

For a young and inexperienced individual to defy societal norms and challenge the wishes of his assertive community was a significant undertaking. Ambalal's courage and unwavering determination sent an unmistakable message about his intention to lead life on his own terms.

However, what is particularly striking is that Ambalal did not seem to extend his strongly progressive ideas to the realm of business. By the turn of the century, Ahmedabad had nearly 20,000 mill workers, with most of the men hailing from the surrounding villages. These mill workers, including those employed in Ambalal's two mills, flocked to the city and established homes in squalid shanties before the Sheths constructed chawls, offering slightly improved but still cramped living conditions. The labour was gruelling, with long hours and minimal time off; workers even worked on Sundays to maintain the machines. The artificially induced dampness inside the mills posed health risks, but there were no provisions for sick leave or medical coverage. While manufacturers had united to form the Millowners Association as early as 1891, the workers were not organised into unions and had limited awareness of their rights.

According to the publicity material released by Ambalal Sarabhai Enterprises, Ambalal is credited with being one of the first employers to support the recognition of trade unions and to establish a hospital for employees as well as a crèche long before such services became legally mandated. However, despite these progressive steps, he did not initiate groundbreaking efforts to improve the plight of the workers or appear to contemplate such initiatives.

However, a challenge to Ambalal's conservatism was brewing, and it would come from within his own family. In 1914, Ambalal's sister, Ansuya, returned to Ahmedabad from England. Originally intending to pursue a medical education, she found herself unable to tolerate the sight of blood and instead became deeply involved in the suffragette movement. Upon her return, she caused quite a stir in Ahmedabad by adopting unconventional habits such as smoking cigarettes and going about with her head uncovered. Ansuya took the initiative to establish a school for the children of millworkers and was deeply dismayed by the deplorable living conditions they endured.

Coincidentally, the following year marked the arrival of a man who would become the city's most distinguished resident—Mohandas Karamchand Gandhi. Stories of the slight, bespectacled advocate trained in England and his crusade against racism in South Africa had preceded his return to India, and he received a tumultuous welcome during his travels across the country. While contemplating potential locations for a new settlement, Gandhi temporarily accepted an offer of a house in Kochrab on the outskirts of Ahmedabad. However, he encountered immediate challenges. His decision to welcome untouchables into his community had sparked outrage in the caste-divided town, leading to a drying up of funds. It was at this crucial juncture that an unidentified individual arrived in a car and made a substantial donation. This anonymous benefactor turned out to be none other than Ambalal himself.

This generous gesture likely raised Gandhi's hopes, as he eventually chose Ahmedabad as his permanent residence, citing the expectation of 'monetary help from its wealthy citizens' as one of his reasons. As anticipated, the affluent mill owners of Ahmedabad not only extended financial support but also became fervent followers of the Mahatma. Gandhi's values of 'non-violence, frugality, honesty, integrity, self-reliance and peace', which closely mirrored their own, endeared him to the Sheths. However, Gandhi's impact on business was unexpected. His 'Swadeshi' campaign protected local mill owners from the competition of imported cloth. Furthermore, his influence on the workforce fostered harmonious labour conditions that would endure for decades to come.

However, this transformation would occur only after a fierce battle, the most bitter confrontation between employers and employees that Ahmedabad had ever witnessed. Ansuya played a pivotal role by approaching Gandhi with a grievance: the mill owners had reneged on a proposed wage increase. Gandhi listened to her complaint and called for a strike.

A strike was an unusual occurrence in the generally mild-mannered city of Ahmedabad, and this one persisted for many weeks. The mill owners, led by Ambalal, stood their ground, refusing to yield. As the workers began to weaken, some returned to their jobs. Sensing the impending defeat, Gandhi embarked on a fast. His rationale was simple: a solution that favoured only one side would not be sustainable. He implored the mill owners to seek a compromise, but they remained resolute and embarrassed. Prominent figures such as Annie Besant, the president of the Indian National Congress, intervened. Under mounting pressure, the mill owners eventually agreed to Gandhi's demand for an impartial arbitrator, leading to a satisfactory resolution. Gandhi ended his fast, and a victory procession saw him, Ambalal and Ansuya driven around in a buggy.

This episode became legendary for several reasons, one of which was the fact that it was here, in this confrontation, that Gandhi first employed the hunger strike as a potent negotiating tool against the British. Erik Erikson, who examined the incident from various angles in his 1970 Pulitzer Prize-winning book

Gandhi's Truth, described the outcome as 'the emergence and the investment of an almost spiritual belief in reconciliation as a ritual'.

The impact of this family history on Vikram was significant. In a speech in 1969, he characterised the experience scientifically as an acknowledgement of the importance of 'frames of reference'. He explained that Gandhi consistently aimed to ensure that in a conflict situation, a solution had to be perceived as right and reasonable from the perspective of both opposing sides. Reconciliation became a prominent theme in Vikram's life, serving as both his strength and his downfall. The episode also garnered attention for the mutual respect displayed by all parties involved in the dispute. Some found Ambalal's tolerance toward his sister incomprehensible and even suggested discontinuing her allowance. However, Ambalal had already demonstrated his resistance to social pressure. Vikram alluded to this trait in a 1970 interview with the BBC, emphasising his family's unconventional values: "All through my childhood, I was brought up to do what one felt was right rather than what society necessarily deemed appropriate."

For Ambalal, the pursuit of 'right', guided by his personal interpretation of the concept, carried the weight of an imperative. He viewed doing what he considered right as simply adhering to his dharma, his moral duty. This perspective also instilled a sense of understatement in both Ambalal and Ansuya, as noted by Erikson. They were reluctant to discuss their individual roles in the historic episode, embodying the principle of nishkama karma—performing tasks without expecting or desiring rewards.

One might have expected that Ambalal's iconoclastic tendencies and religious inclinations would deter him from indulging in material pleasures. However, Ambalal's personal philosophy encouraged an almost deliberate embrace of the good life. Photographs from the 1910s and 1920s depict the family dressed in the height of fashion: Ambalal in a Saville Row suit, his wife Sarla in a high-collared blouse and sari adorned with an embroidered border, surrounded by their children in various outfits, overseen by a formidable English governess who was well-dressed and adorned with lace at her neck and a stylish hat.

Until 1920, the Sarabhais moved between various cities. They briefly resided in a three-storied house called Malden Hall on Marine Lines in Bombay, where they furnished their home with furniture from fashionable European stores like Wimbric and Benjamin. They enjoyed rides on the beach and evenings at clubs. Ambalal's business often took him to England, and the entire family accompanied him, establishing a residence in Hampstead complete with two cars and silver tableware. However, finding suitable schooling for their growing family proved challenging, as none of the educational institutions in the places they lived aligned with Ambalal's idealistic notions or those of his wife.

Sarla Devi, formerly known as Rewa, was the daughter of a widower, Harilal Ghosalia, an advocate and a 'self-made man' with somewhat Victorian views, influenced by Kant and Hegel. Despite being frugal and deeply religious—she modelled herself after Rama's faithful consort, Sita—Rewa possessed a streak of independence uncommon for her time and had received an English education. Ambalal was reportedly impressed by her boldness during their initial meeting and chose her as his wife, despite the evident disparities in their material circumstances.

Ambalal and Rewa shared many commonalities, which made them well-suited for each other. Both had experienced early responsibilities in their lives. Rewa had taken on a parental role with her siblings, managed a household, and provided companionship to her father. This combination of maturity and idealism likely enabled her to respond positively to Ambalal's unconventional courtship. During their engagement period, the couple exchanged letters that openly discussed various expectations for their married life, which was quite unusual for the times. In Sarla (Rewa), Ambalal had found a partner in his pursuit of constructing an 'ideal' life.

Fortuitously, as they contemplated the future of their growing family, they came across a review of a new book on child-rearing in the Times Literary Supplement. This book, authored by Maria Montessori, an Italian physicist, presented a revolutionary system of primary education with the motto:'First the education of the senses, then the education of the intellect'. Montessori's system emphasised self-determination and self-realisation and had been tested through the establishment of a children's home (Casa dei Bambini) in Rome in 1907.

The Sarabhais read Montessori's book while sailing back from England, and its contents resonated deeply with their vague yearnings and unarticulated thoughts on education. This discovery inspired them to put Montessori's 'radical yet convincing' ideas into practice by starting their own Casa dei Bambini in Ahmedabad.

Financial constraints were not an issue for them, as they were financially capable of pursuing their vision. Ambalal had become one of the most prominent figures in the community of mill owners and had established himself as a savvy businessman. His business ventures included importing machinery and techniques from Lancashire, making Calico a pioneer in fine cloth production, and engaging in various enterprises such as a sugar factory in Bihar, a railway line in East Bengal, borax import from Tibet, cotton ginning factories in East Africa, and a trading office in London. Some of these ventures were in partnership with his cousin's husband and close friend, Babubhai. Ambalal's impressive stature was complemented by his fine suits and brand of cigarettes with his name embossed in gold. He was also the proud owner of the city's first car and had relocated his family to a 21-acre estate in Shahibaug known as 'The Retreat', reflecting the colonial style of the era.

Ambalal's relocation to 'The Retreat' in Shahibaug was a move befitting his status. This area, steeped in history, was originally established in the 17th century by Shah Jahan, then serving as the viceroy of Ahmedabad. Known as Prince Khurram at the time, Shah Jahan built Shahibaug as a royal garden palace, showcasing his aesthetic sensibilities that would later culminate in the creation of the Taj Mahal. The palace, surrounded by a traditional Mughal charbagh, symbolised the pinnacle of 17th-century Indian garden design. Over time, as the Mughal Empire faded, Shahibaug's glory diminished, setting the stage for affluent individuals like Ambalal to infuse new life into this historic locale.

Building on Ambalal's move to Shahibaug, by the 19th century, the once magnificent garden palace had fallen into decay following the decline of the Mughal Empire. The commoners remained within the city walls in densely packed, intricately designed neighbourhoods known as pols. It was during this period that wealthy industrialists, known as Sheths, began to discover Shahibaug. Seeking alternatives to the cramped pols, these Sheths were drawn to the vast open spaces of Shahibaug, which once hosted royalty. Their newfound wealth from mill operations allowed them to build grand homes there, inspired by the architectural styles of Gujarat and Saurashtra's princely clans.

Ambalal, himself a figure of prominence, was part of this transformative era. He inherited a substantial 21-acre estate in Shahibaug, known as 'The Retreat', from his uncle Chimanbhai, who had constructed a bungalow there in 1904. This move from Shantisadan, the joint family home in the city, to 'The Retreat' marked a significant change in Ambalal's life, reflecting his rising stature and the shifting preferences of Ahmedabad's elite. 'The

Retreat', with its colonial-style architecture, not only symbolised Ambalal's affluence but also mirrored the broader transition of Shahibaug from a royal garden to a symbol of industrial wealth and modernity.

Continuing from Ambalal's relocation to 'The Retreat', the community of Shahibaug was characterised by a network of wealthy families, often interconnected through marriage and other social ties. This elite group, known as the Sheths, included notable families like the Parsi Vakils and the Lalbhais, each contributing to the cultural and economic fabric of the area.

The Parsi Vakils, who resided to the left of 'The Retreat' across the police lines, were among the early affluent settlers in Shahibaug, even predating the Sarabhais. One prominent member of this community, Cowasjee Vakil, played a vital role in the city's development. He was known for his brick-making business, which supplied materials for much of old Ahmedabad's construction, including significant structures like the Calico Mills.

Adjacent to 'The Retreat' was Lalbaug, the residence of Chimanbhai Lalbhai. The Lalbhai family, renowned for their industrial and philanthropic endeavours, had close ties with the Sarabhais. This relationship was further cemented through matrimonial alliances, as Chimanbhai's daughter Manorama married Ambalal's eldest son, Suhrid. Additionally, Kasturbhai Lalbhai, Chimanbhai's brother and a celebrated philanthropist-industrialist, was a key collaborator and loyal ally of Vikram Sarabhai. These familial and business connections among the Sheths of Shahibaug not only shaped the social landscape of the area but also influenced the economic and cultural development of Ahmedabad.

In 1919, Shahibaug presented a stark contrast to its new developments, remaining a vast expanse of dark terrain adjacent to the Sabarmati River. This river, typically arid, transformed into a raging torrent during monsoons, frequently overflowing its banks. The landscape was punctuated by historical wells dating back to the Mughal era and shaded by dirt paths.

Each evening, the area resonated with the distinct sound of a siren, heralding the end of the day for factory workers. Notably, the properties of local Sheths were located along a prominent road. This road, leading towards a palace and a military cantonment, also meandered past a dilapidated Hanuman temple, now a haven for lively monkeys.

In the midst of this rustic setting, Ambalal Sarabhai envisioned and brought to life his personal paradise, aptly named 'Eden'. The grand entrance to this estate was marked by towering gates, opening onto a lengthy driveway leading to a unique three-storied structure crowned with a turret.

This architectural marvel skillfully blended Indian and European design sensibilities, evident in its simple yet elegant lines and tastefully crafted interiors. Designed for comfort in the intense summer heat, each of the 50-odd rooms was equipped with electric fans and shutters.

The extensive property not only housed the main residence but also featured various outhouses, garages, a swimming pool, and courts for badminton, croquet, and cricket. A dedicated team of twenty hamals, six bais, two cooks, thirty gardeners, and ten guards, along with numerous drivers and cleaners, diligently maintained this miniature township. Additional amenities included a laundry area, cowshed, and stables, each stable housing a horse for every family member.

'The Retreat', as it was known, also boasted a rich tapestry of flora and fauna. Exotic animals and birds roamed freely across its vast grounds, which were adorned with an array of trees, flowers, Greek statues, including a replica of the Venus De Milo, and tranquil lily ponds.

It was within this idyllic setting that Vikram Sarabhai entered the world on 12 August 1919. His sister Leena Mangaldas recounts this event in her book Akhand Divo. The siblings, already five in number—Mridula, Bharti, Suhrid, Gautam, and Leena—were out on a drive when their syce, Salim Khan, beckoned them home with news of their newborn brother. Eagerly, they rushed back, ascending to the third floor to meet the fair, large-foreheaded, and big-eared infant, whimsically contemplating folding his ears into paan shapes.

❑

Strange But Unique Educational Background

Vikram Sarabhai, in his toddler years, was notably energetic and adventurous. A memorable incident occurred on a steamer trip when he vanished, only to be found later in the hold at Port Said. Ted Standing, who spent time in Ahmedabad and recorded his experiences in a diary, remembered Vikram for his 'large head and big beautiful brown eyes'.

In his diary, Standing captured vivid images of the Sarabhai children. He noted that Vikram, having recently mastered walking, was keen to explore, often embarking on little adventures. Vikram was always followed by a silent yet dignified figure, his 'faithful angel', who would gracefully assist him whenever he encountered trouble.

The other Sarabhai children each had their unique traits. Mridula was seen as mature beyond her years; Bharti was precocious with a spark of genius. Suhrid embodied the quintessential inquisitive boy, while Gautam was quiet yet enterprising, always eager to participate. Leena, with her dark eyes, was known for her playful and mischievous demeanour. The youngest siblings, Gita and Gira, were not yet born at this time.

The family also had pets, including a bull terrier named Tippie, known for his calm temperament and friendly nature, and puppies with whimsical names like Robin, Gipsy and Charlie Chaplin.

The Sarabhai children were the sole students at a new school established at 'The Retreat', a decision made after careful consideration by the Sarabhais about whether to include children from outside the family. This choice reflected the broader changes occurring in Ahmedabad, where educational institutions were burgeoning, social reform was gaining momentum, and discussions on topics like women's education and scientific discoveries were commonplace. The emergence of a moderate-sized middle and intellectual class was also noted, partly driven by opportunities with the East India Company.

Despite their respect within the community, especially after Ambalal's role in a textile strike, the Sarabhais faced scepticism about their progressive views. For instance, when Ambalal named a hospital wing after his wife in 1918, it elicited critical commentary from the local magazine Praja Bandh, highlighting the city's discomfort with his modern ideas.

Ambalal Sarabhai's personality was marked by bluntness and a strong sense of individualism, traits that were not always well-received outside his immediate circle. Ushaben, the daughter of writer Dhumketu, acknowledged the Sarabhais as a prominent Ahmedabad family but also pointed out their whimsical nature. Similarly, Pranlal Patel, a photographer who often visited the family for events, had mixed feelings about them.

After much deliberation, the Sarabhais concluded that their school at 'The Retreat' would be exclusively for their eight children. Leena, one of the Sarabhais, rationalised this decision, suggesting that it would have been unfair to involve others in what was essentially an experimental educational venture. This sentiment was echoed by CJBhatt, a teacher at the school, who remarked on the bold and unorthodox nature of the endeavour. He pointed out the absence of a conventional framework or trained personnel for this new educational approach, likening it to venturing into uncharted waters.

The Sarabhais' quest for an ideal educational setting was marked by a certain rigidity in their expectations. Both Ambalal and Sarla Sarabhai were known for their intolerance towards anything that did not align with their high standards. They envisioned for their children an education that was not just about academics but an all-encompassing experience. They aimed to create a nurturing and stimulating environment, a 'hothouse' filled with diverse educational stimuli, designed to foster comprehensive learning and development.

Miss Williams, a teacher who had travelled from London to join the faculty at 'The Retreat', was struck by the extraordinary commitment of the Sarabhais to their children's education. In records, she is referred to only by her last name, but her words carry significant weight. She remarked that she had never read or dreamt of parents as devoted to their children's education as the Sarabhais. This level of dedication was not just an anecdote but was evident in the very scale and setup of the school.

The investment in the school was apparent, not just in financial terms but also in the unwavering resolve and clarity of vision. There was no room for doubt or half-measures in the Sarabhais' educational venture. This was further exemplified by the quality of the teachers they hired. The educators brought to 'The Retreat' were of a high calibre, reflecting the seriousness with which Sarla Sarabhai, in particular, approached the educational mission. Her dedication was so profound that Maria Montessori, the renowned Italian educator, referred to her as the 'ideal Montessori mother', highlighting her deep alignment with the Montessori educational philosophy.

The Retreat's educational landscape was enriched by a diverse and highly qualified team of about a dozen teachers. This team included three PhD holders and three graduates from various European universities. The faculty was further bolstered by respected local educators like Karuna Shanker, who imparted knowledge in Sanskrit, the Cambridge-educated mathematician SH Gidwani, and the renowned poet Dhumketu. Specialised instructors were also appointed for music and sports, demonstrating the school's commitment to a well-rounded education. In an instance of uncompromising pursuit of quality, Sarla Sarabhai, dissatisfied with the local dancing teacher, promptly arranged for a replacement from Santiniketan, a prestigious Bengali cultural centre.

The curriculum at 'The Retreat' was exceptionally broad and inclusive, covering languages like Gujarati, Sanskrit, Hindi, English and Bengali. Academic subjects such as history, geography, mathematics, physics and chemistry were complemented by artistic disciplines including drawing, painting, dancing, music, pottery, handicrafts and sculpture. The school also catered to athletic interests, offering lessons in badminton, tennis, riding, archery and yoga. Artistic students had access to a variety of musical instruments, including the sitar, veena, dilruba, violin and tabla.

In this unique educational setting, there was a seamless integration of work and play. Students were encouraged to engage in practical life skills, assisting in the aviary, kitchen and cowshed, managing finances, and hosting guests. This approach fostered a sense of responsibility and real-world understanding among the students.

The overarching philosophy of 'The Retreat's' educational system was the absence of compulsion.

JS Badami, a teacher at the school, emphasised that the primary role of educators was to ignite a passion for knowledge in the pupils, rather than merely transmitting information. This philosophy extended to assessments as well. The students took examinations through the government-run RC High School, but only when they were individually assessed as ready for matriculation, prioritising each child's unique developmental timeline over a standardised educational model.

Life at 'The Retreat' was a unique blend of structured discipline and the enjoyment of sensory experiences. Each day commenced early, with the entire household rising by six o'clock. Mornings were bustling with activities, including singing, painting, spinning, weaving and archery. Some would start their day with a visit to the library or workshop. The formal school day began at seven, accompanied by servings of cocoa, a comforting ritual for the children.

Ambalal Sarabhai, deeply involved in his business ventures like setting up the Swastik Oil Mills in Bombay, ensured he spared moments for familial interaction. Whenever he was at 'The Retreat', he made it a point to visit the school area in the mornings to greet everyone, adding a personal touch to the day.

The children's recreational life was equally vibrant. Toys, often wrapped in large cloth parcels, were regularly delivered to 'The Retreat', bringing excitement and new playthings to explore. Additionally, every Saturday was marked by the arrival of comics from England, an eagerly awaited treat. Sundays were special too, often featuring pool parties that welcomed guests, creating a sense of community and leisure.

Social interactions for the Sarabhai children were not limited to their immediate family. They frequently mingled with the neighbouring Lalbhai children. Vikram and Gautam, in particular, enjoyed spending time in the Lalbhai's playhouse. The boys also organised cricket matches, which included participation from the gardeners' sons and their teachers, fostering a sense of camaraderie.

The Sarabhai children's exposure to cultural events was a priority. They attended garden parties, complete with live bands and strawberry drinks, making for memorable experiences. For exceptional occasions, such as performances by renowned artists like the Russian dancer Anna Pavlova, the family would make special trips to Bombay, ensuring the children had exposure to global arts and culture.

Vacations were an integral part of the Sarabhai children's upbringing, considered crucial for their education. These were not just simple trips; they were elaborate excursions to various destinations like Mussoorie, Simla, Shillong, Kashmir, Ooty, Ceylon, Mount Abu and Matheran. Accompanying the family on these journeys were a retinue of servants, pets, and their entire team of teachers, making these vacations a massive undertaking. An advance party was often sent ahead to ensure that all arrangements were in place, showcasing the level of planning and commitment to these educational travels.

Ambalal Sarabhai was the architect behind the meticulously planned family trips, showcasing his skills as a resourceful organiser. He was attentive to the smallest of details, ensuring the family's luggage was easily identifiable by painting signs in bright yellow. Ambalal also took the initiative to prepare lists of vegetarian meals, contacting restaurants in advance to accommodate the family's dietary preferences.

Mrinalini Sarabhai, Vikram's wife, reflected on the family dynamics, noting the paramount importance the parents placed on their children. "The parents kept the children above everything. They were utterly cared for, completely cherished," she observed. In a society traditionally governed by patriarchal norms, Ambalal stood out for his acute sensitivity towards his children's needs and emotions.

Even during his frequent absences, Ambalal made concerted efforts to maintain a strong bond with his family. He creatively kept in touch by writing TirangiSamachar, a whimsical daily newsletter that added a touch of humour and connection despite the physical distance. A poignant example of his care was highlighted by Leena Sarabhai, who recalled a distressing incident when her pet mongrel went missing during a train journey. Ambalal's response was immediate and thorough; he not only sent a servant to search for the lost pet but also placed an advertisement offering a reward for its safe return.

This nurturing environment played a significant role in shaping Vikram Sarabhai's character, particularly his remarkable ability to trust. Ashis Nandy, a psychoanalyst acquainted with the family, opined that Vikram's trusting nature was a direct result of the gentle and secure upbringing he received. Nandy believed Vikram to have been a deeply desired child, reflecting the intense emotional investment of his parents.

However, there was an element of disproportion in Ambalal's extreme solicitude for his family. His involvement in even the most minor aspects of travel planning suggested an obsessive attention to detail. This trait, later seen in Vikram, indicated a certain fastidiousness. The unquestioned assumptions underlying Ambalal's relationship with his children sometimes bordered on the excessive. Mrinalini Sarabhai shared a story that vividly illustrated this aspect of Ambalal's parenting, highlighting both its depth and its complexity.

During a family vacation in England, a young Vikram Sarabhai, around six or seven years old, was captivated by a toy he saw and expressed his desire for it. Ambalal Sarabhai, ever the considerate father, explained to Vikram that he was running short on funds, but promised that if he had any money left at the end of their trip, he would purchase the toy for him. Vikram appeared content with this promise, and the matter slipped into the background as their travels continued.

It wasn't until their ship docked at Brindisi, Italy, for refuelling, that Vikram remembered the toy and inquired with his father about it. Realising he had indeed forgotten but had sufficient funds remaining, Ambalal, quite earnestly, offered to take Vikram back to England to fulfil his promise and purchase the toy. However, in a display of maturity that belied his young age, Vikram declined the offer, and the family proceeded with their journey.

This anecdote, as recounted by Mrinalini Sarabhai, Vikram's wife, serves to illustrate the profound respect Ambalal held for his commitments, even those made to his children. The incident reveals the unique values in the Sarabhai household, where a father's readiness to undertake an extravagant gesture was met with a child's remarkably mature and composed refusal.

The family dynamics in the Sarabhai household were perhaps influenced by Ambalal's own upbringing, with a tendency towards reversing traditional parent-child roles. This aspect of their family life, as Mrinalini's story indicates, contributed significantly to Vikram's early maturity.

Additionally, the Jain roots of the Sarabhai family subtly influenced their day-to-day practices, though they were not overtly religious. The children's schooldays would commence with a few minutes of silent meditation, accommodating the diverse spiritual beliefs of the faculty. Vikram, in his later years, mentioned in a letter and a television interview his personal approach to religion and vegetarianism, which was less about religious doctrine and more about aesthetics and ethical considerations, particularly the aversion to killing.

This philosophy extended even to the family's dietary habits, with strict adherence to Jain life-preserving rituals. The Sarabhais, including their pets, adhered to a vegetarian diet. A daily ritual in the household involved placing a saucer of milk outside for ants, demonstrating their commitment to non-violence and respect for all living beings.

The lifestyle at 'The Retreat', though idyllic, refined, and filled with a sense of purpose and aesthetic satisfaction, was not without its critics. This unique way of living, while cherished within the family, occasionally led to discomfort or misunderstanding among those less acquainted with their unconventional approach.

Ted Standing, while appreciating the ideals of his hosts at 'The Retreat', once made a comparison in his writings that vividly captured the essence of the place. He likened the compound, with its enchanting fairy lights and elegant alabaster statues, to the luxurious enclosure described in The Light of Asia,where the young prince Siddhartha was kept isolated from the harsh realities of life, such as disease and death. This parallel drawn by Standing also highlighted his internal conflict, as he grappled with feelings of guilt about the stark contrast between the opulence within 'The Retreat' and the 'incredible squalor' experienced by thousands living beyond its high walls.

The environment of 'The Retreat', especially in its early days, was notably serene and insulated from the harsher aspects of reality, such as poverty and violence. Leena Sarabhai recalled the harmonious nature of their family life, marked by an absence of shouting, abuse, or fighting. This peaceful atmosphere extended to the behaviour of the children, who were often observed to be remarkably polite towards their elders and each other.

Despite their individual preferences and quirks, such as Bharti's fondness for silks and brogues or Gira's tomboyish tendencies, the Sarabhai children managed to navigate their formative years without the typical familial conflicts. Kartikeya Sarabhai, reflecting on his grandmother's influence, noted how she instilled in her children the belief that the Sarabhais were distinct from others, with an emphasis on avoiding feelings of jealousy and hatred. However, he also acknowledged that this approach had its drawbacks, especially for those who did experience these emotions but were unsure how to process them.

The suppression of certain negative emotions among the children at 'The Retreat' could sometimes have unintended consequences. Leena wrote about two such incidents: one where she deliberately hit her aunt with a poisonous weed and another where she threw sand into the piano used by Ambalal for evening musical sessions. Both actions were later recounted with a sense of remorse and confusion, indicating a struggle to understand the origin of such impulsive behaviours within the disciplined and controlled environment of 'The Retreat'.

Within the tranquil confines of 'The Retreat', certain subjects remained unspoken, creating an atmosphere of implicit taboos that lingered in the air. One such subject was sex, which was not broached until the children had surpassed adolescence. Even then, as Leena Sarabhai emphasised, discussions were conducted with a strict avoidance of coarseness or vulgarity. This restraint extended to the overall tone of interactions within the household. Captain Lakshmi Sehgal, Mrinalini Sarabhai's sister and a renowned freedom fighter, distinctly remembered the absence of humour and liveliness, particularly around the dinner table, a stark contrast to the typical boisterousness of family gatherings.

Natural fears also permeated the environment at 'The Retreat'. Despite the dedicated efforts of two gardeners tasked with keeping monkeys at bay, these creatures frequently disrupted the tranquillity with their noisy chatter and movements on the rooftops. The large, imposing house had its share of unwelcome inhabitants too, including lizards and bugs. A vivid memory for Vikram was being bitten on the eyelid by one of these insects, resulting in a swollen, black eye that lasted for days. The presence of death also loomed over the household, adding a sombre note to their existence.

The Sarabhai family was no stranger to loss and mourning. Kanta, whose death left a profound impact, continued to be a poignant, almost spectral presence in the family, kept alive by Ambalal's deep-seated remorse. Later, the family grappled with the passing of Babubhai, Ambalal's close friend and business partner, who was also married to Ambalal's cousin, Nirmala. Babubhai's death was a significant emotional blow, yet outward expressions of grief were not encouraged, compelling Ambalal to suppress his sorrow.

This trait of restrained emotional expression was inherited by the Sarabhai children. Leena's son, Kamal Mangaldas, an architect, recollected his mother's reaction to the news of her own mother's passing. When informed, Leena briefly allowed herself a sob before regaining composure, ready to face the responsibilities that lay ahead.

In retrospect, the Sarabhai family experiment with its unconventional upbringing seems to have had mixed outcomes. As adults, each sibling achieved excellence in their respective fields. Bharti Sarabhai earned accolades from TS Eliot for her playwriting, Gautam Sarabhai established the National Institute of Design and the BM Institute of Mental Health, and Leena Sarabhai founded the Shreyas School. Gita Sarabhai pursued her passion for music and drama, while Gira Sarabhai was recognised for her work with the renowned Textile Museum.

Despite the affluence and unconventional upbringing in the Sarabhai household, the personal lives of the siblings, as they grew older, were marked by a series of challenges. The family, known for its near-teetotaler lifestyle, faced unexpected issues like alcoholism. Moreover, several of the siblings experienced failed marriages, further marring the image of an otherwise illustrious family. These personal struggles were accompanied by an overarching reputation for eccentricity that seemed to shroud the family.

Kamal Mangaldas, a member of the extended family, offered a candid assessment of the Sarabhai siblings. He observed that, with a few exceptions, many of them tended to be self-centred and inept at forming and maintaining human relationships. This self-admitted flaw in the family dynamics was reflective of the complexities beneath the surface of their privileged life.

The decline of the family was further exacerbated by the collapse of their business. In the aftermath of the educational experiment at 'The Retreat', the family's business ventures faltered. The subsequent division of assets became a source of profound bitterness, fragmenting the once-united family.

'The Retreat' itself, once a hub of familial warmth and activity, underwent a significant transformation. It was converted into a museum, a repository of paintings and antiques. This change in function from a bustling family home to a museum open only by appointment symbolised the shift in the family's dynamics.

The isolation within the family was physically manifested in the way several members built their own separate houses within the expansive grounds of 'The Retreat'. Each dwelling reflected the individual's personality and interests, from Gautam's elaborately carved mud house adorned with earthenware animals to Gira's modest abode surrounded by exotic trees. Leena's penchant for rearing unusual animals added to the unique ambiance of the estate, now resplendent with peacocks.

Khushwant Singh, during his visit, observed these individualistic tendencies. He noted the once-weekly family meals, the only occasion when all members gathered together. However, the underlying fractures were evident; when the family split, communication between members ceased, and the family business rapidly deteriorated.

In contrast to this narrative of familial discord and individual pursuits, two siblings, Mridula and Vikram Sarabhai, charted a different course. Distancing themselves from the familial enclave at an early age, they immersed themselves in public life. Their commitment to broader societal issues and mass-based ideals, starkly different from their siblings' more insular interests, was a testament to the influence of their unique upbringing. Their paths highlighted a different aspect of the Sarabhai legacy, one that was outward-looking and engaged with wider societal concerns.

Vikram Sarabhai and his elder sister Mridula presented a study in contrasts. Mridula, with her short hair and gruff voice, was perceived as a tough rebel by both her family and the people of Ahmedabad. Known affectionately as 'boss' within the family and referred to as 'Pathan' by the awed locals, her rebellious nature manifested early. As a child, she boldly ate with the Harijans and often chose the cheap seats in cinema halls, steadfastly refusing to move even when the cinema owner, recognising her, offered her an upgrade. This strong sense of justice eventually led her to the freedom struggle, where, as Khushwant Singh noted, she exhibited remarkable fearlessness and courage.

Post-independence, however, Mridula's defiance sometimes caused discomfort among her friends. MO Mathai, Nehru's private secretary, once described her as possessing both the courage and the recklessness of a wild boar. She even faced allegations of cruelty towards Partition refugees. Her behaviour occasionally bordered on the erratic; a neighbour recalled an incident where Mridula emerged with a whip to frighten a taxi driver who had overcharged her. Despite these attributes, Mridula, during her younger years, was known to be a caring sibling who looked after her brothers and sisters, especially the young Vikram.

Vikram, as an infant, was notably good-looking with a large forehead, delicate features, and protruding ears. Photographs from his childhood show him in various outfits, from shorts and a sailor suit to a traditional white jabho with mojdis, his long, straight hair often falling over his eyes. His pictures suggest a compliant nature, rarely smiling but always gazing intently at the camera, a slight wrinkle above his nose hinting at deeper thoughts. His sister Gita described him as having his own private world, being part of the family yet somehow distinct. Mallika, Vikram's daughter, later characterised him as a perpetual thinker, often seen with his chin on his hands, reminiscent of Rodin's The Thinker.

Leena, Vikram's elder sister, fondly remembered his childhood attachment to his toy train. He was inseparable from it, taking it to bed, and even talking to it while on the potty. Gita recalled his early interest in Manipuri dance and the sitar. Vikram also had a mischievous side; he would tease his siblings by rapidly reciting verses from the Ramayana.

Vikram's intellectual prowess was evident from an early age. JS Badami, in his diary, remarked on Vikram's exceptional intellectual awareness and the early blossoming of his integrated personality, rare even among geniuses. He noted Vikram's comprehensive pursuit of knowledge and his unique originality and keen observation, evident in the questions he asked, even as a young child.

Vikram Sarabhai's childhood at 'The Retreat' was not just about refinement and education; it also involved robust physical activities. He enthusiastically engaged in cricket and boating, often ending up in the lake's waters with a laugh. His skill in cycling was notable; he delighted in performing a circus-like trick where he would ride at high speed, lift his hands and feet, cross his arms, and place his feet on the handlebars, sometimes even daring to close his eyes on straight roads, much to the concern of the household staff.

The narrative of Vikram Sarabhai's early years includes two incidents that have often been recounted. The first involves Rabindranath Tagore, who visited Ahmedabad in 1920 and stayed with the Sarabhais, including a month-long visit to Shillong. Tagore, an admirer of phrenology, observed Vikram's large and distinctively shaped forehead and is said to have remarked to Sarla Sarabhai, "This boy will achieve great things." This prediction by the revered poet laureate underscored the early signs of Vikram's potential.

Another anecdote from Vikram's childhood occurred during a family holiday. Ambalal Sarabhai noticed his son receiving mail on family stationery and inquired about the frequent correspondence. Vikram's innocent response that he was writing to himself hinted at a reflective and perhaps introspective nature.

While these stories might suggest a propensity for precociousness, Vikram, as a child, did not exhibit such traits overtly. In a family of distinct personalities, each pursuing their own significant causes, as Erik Erikson later described, it was challenging for any one child to dominate the spotlight. Vikram, in particular, seemed to inherit his father Ambalal's introspective qualities, remaining a relatively quiet child.

Vikram shared a deep bond with his mother and remained affectionate throughout his life. His sisters recalled how he would rest his head in her lap, maintaining a childlike interaction with her even in adulthood. This display of physical affection was somewhat unusual, given the general perception of Sarla Sarabhai as being somewhat reserved. Kamal Mangaldas contrasted his interactions with his grandparents, noting he never touched his grandmother, whereas he would climb onto his grandfather's shoulders and playfully pat his head. Ambalal Sarabhai, in contrast to Sarla, was seen as less austere and more jovial. Navroz Contractor, a family friend, remembered Ambalal's spontaneous support for a cricket pitch and his enthusiastic involvement in watching the games, often inquiring light-heartedly about their performance.

Vikram Sarabhai, in his formative years at 'The Retreat', exhibited a blend of his parents' traits. Unlike his mother Sarla's straightforward rigidity, Vikram leaned more towards his father

Ambalal's complex and nuanced approach to life. Sarla, a devout Gujarati housewife, adhered to regular religious practices, including daily worship and organising a Satyanarayan puja every fortnight, a ritual she inherited from her mother. Ambalal, on the other hand, while maintaining a private shrine, delved deeper into the philosophical aspects of his faith. Uncharacteristically for him, he didn't hesitate to break traditional rules if he deemed it practical.

This pragmatic approach of Ambalal was evident in 1915 whenfaced with a rabies outbreak in the Calico Mills compound, he ordered all stray dogs to be shot, igniting controversy within the community. His unflinching decision-making was again on display in 1919 when, at Gandhi's request, he assisted in euthanising a sick calf at Sabarmati Ashram, leading to severe criticism from Jains who unfavourably compared him to Brigadier-General Reginald Dyer of the Jallianwala Bagh massacre.

Vikram inherited this pragmatic streak from his father. Often portrayed as a pacifist and a Gandhian, Vikram's worldview was more nuanced, capable of understanding and navigating the moral greys of various situations, much like his father's.

The intellectual and cultural milieu at 'The Retreat' further enriched Vikram's upbringing. The Sarabhai home was a hub for some of the era's most brilliant minds. Eminent figures like Rabindranath Tagore, physicist Jagadish Chandra Bose, historian Jadunath Sarkar, Nobel laureate CV Raman, Bharatanatyam dancer Rukmini Arundale, philosopher J Krishnamurti, and actor Prithviraj Kapoor were frequent guests. This exposure to diverse and influential personalities played a significant role in shaping his perspectives.

'The Retreat' also hosted political luminaries, drawn by Gandhi's presence in Ahmedabad. Dignitaries like Dadasaheb Mavlankar, Madan Mohan Malaviya, Sardar Patel, Maulana Azad, Sarojini Naidu, CF Andrews, Muhammad Ali Jinnah, and Dr S Radhakrishnan were among the many who visited. The Sarabhais shared a particularly close bond with the Nehru family; Motilal and Jawaharlal Nehru stayed at 'The Retreat', and when Jawaharlal's daughter Indira moved to Poona for her studies, Ambalal and Sarla took it upon themselves to look after her. These connections, rich in cultural and political significance, were to prove invaluable for Vikram in his later years.

In this environment, Vikram's growth was marked by a unique blend of his father's philosophical pragmatism, his exposure to leading thinkers and political figures, and the influence of his mother's devout practices, all contributing to the multifaceted personality he was to become.

The illustrious list of guests at 'The Retreat' might give an impression that the Sarabhais were indulging in the wealthy elite's hobby of gathering famous personalities. However, their involvement with these distinguished individuals went beyond mere social hosting. The Sarabhai family was deeply engaged in the Indian freedom movement, a commitment far surpassing the role of conventional hosts.

Mahatma Gandhi was a significant figure in shaping the Sarabhais' involvement in the freedom struggle. Despite an earlier confrontation with Gandhi during the textile strike, Ambalal's respect and admiration for Gandhi remained unshaken. In 1918, Ambalal and Sarla even invited Gandhi to their home for recuperation from a serious illness. Gandhi himself acknowledged the exceptional care he received during his stay, highlighting the depth of service and affection he experienced.

Sarla's inclination towards simplicity, which led her to forsake her silks for plain white cotton, was attributed by some to the influence of Gandhi, while others believed it was a response to the death of her eldest son. Her devout nature resonated with Gandhi, who affectionately referred to her as his 'sister'. He even nominated her as a trustee of the All-India Spinning

Association, a proposal met with resistance due to her status as the wife of a 'textile king'. Undeterred, Gandhi entrusted her with the leadership of the Kasturba Gandhi National Memorial Trust in Gujarat. The Sarabhai family soon found themselves deeply immersed in the freedom movement.

The year after Vikram's birth, in 1920, Gandhi's call for the non-cooperation movement on the eve of the Prince of Wales's visit ignited a fervent nationalistic spirit across the country. His impassioned plea for resistance against British rule stirred the nation. As recounted by Raj Thapar, wife of journalist Romesh Thapar, this period was marked by a collective eagerness to challenge British tyranny and to reclaim 'national honour', even though many, especially the youth, were still grasping the full meaning and implications of this monumental struggle.

In this context, the Sarabhai household stood as a beacon of both intellectual engagement and active participation in the freedom movement, their role extending far beyond the confines of wealthy socialites to significant contributors in India's struggle for independence.

At 'The Retreat', the struggle for India's freedom was intensely personal and deeply felt. The women of the Sarabhai family were at the forefront of this movement, actively participating in various activities, often at great personal risk. Vikram's aunts, Indumati and Nirmalaben, were pivotal in establishing the city's first khadi store. Sarla, along with Mridula, spearheaded the boycott of foreign cloth and the picketing of liquor shops, tasks fraught with danger due to the nature of the opposition. Mridula, known for her fearlessness, famously stopped a liquor consignment by grabbing the reins of a horse, an act that not only made her a local legend but also inspired many young women to join the satyagraha.

The freedom movement permeated the daily life at 'The Retreat'. In a household renowned for its textile manufacturing, khaddar, or homespun cloth, became a symbol of defiance and choice. Mridula and Ansuya went as far as to use khaddar for curtains and bedclothes. Influenced by the prevailing atmosphere and regularly reading Gandhi's magazine Harijan, Vikram and his sister Gita also adopted khaddar.

One of Vikram's most vivid childhood experiences was the Dandi March. At 11 years old, he witnessed the historic event when Gandhi set out to defy the British salt laws. The Sarabhai family, along with thousands of others, gathered at Sabarmati Ashram on the eve of the march. The prayer meeting that night was particularly moving, setting the stage for Gandhi's 200-mile journey to the sea, a journey marked by growing crowds and celebratory villages, culminating in a potent act of civil disobedience.

The increasing confrontations with the British authorities and the frequent arrests of family members profoundly impacted the Sarabhai children. Vikram, in a French television documentary, recalled the police confiscating property from their home as a penalty for relatives in jail, a consequence of Ambalal's refusal to pay fines in line with the non-cooperation movement. Gita, two years younger than Vikram, expressed a deep sense of loss and the shift from a carefree childhood to a more sombre reality when their mother was taken away by the police.

The close association with Gandhi left an indelible mark on Vikram. His colleagues later noted his deep engagement with Gandhian economics, suggesting a strong influence of Gandhi's ideals on him. Vikram himself, in the French documentary, spoke with reverence and admiration about Gandhi. He fondly remembered the prayer meetings at Sabarmati Ashram, the beautiful Sanskrit chants, and a particularly meaningful conversation with Gandhi about communal issues, highlighting how Gandhi's willingness to engage with him, a young boy, made a lasting impression.

Surrounded by the fervour of the Indian freedom movement, Vikram Sarabhai, then a teenager in the 1930s, remarkably remained detached from the struggle. This was a period when even children, referred to as 'vanar senas', were actively involved in the movement, echoing the patriotic spirit through various activities. Vikram's contemporary, Prabhaben, who was to marry his neighbour and friend, Chinubhai, reminisced about engaging in acts of defiance as a child. Yet, despite growing up in such a charged atmosphere, there is no evidence to suggest that Vikram ever considered joining the freedom struggle, whether in Ahmedabad, during his time at Cambridge, or upon his return.

One plausible explanation for Vikram's apparent disinterest in the freedom movement could be his foresight and focus on the future of post-independence India. He seemed to understand early on that his strengths lay in the realms of education and technology, and that he could make a more significant contribution in these areas rather than in the political turbulence of the time. Throughout his life, Vikram's public speeches were devoid of references to contemporary events or controversies, reflecting his long-term visionary approach.

Vikram's childhood was marked by a profound love for science. His schoolteacher, CJ Bhatt, noted his strong inclination towards the pure sciences. This early interest was evident in his fascination with a toy set named Junero, which allowed him to create various metal designs. Further nurturing his scientific curiosity, Vikram, with the help of Khimjibhai Mistry, a carpenter, built a functional steam engine large enough to ride. Photographs from that time show a young Vikram proudly posing with the engine and its creators.

Recognising their son's penchant for mechanics, Vikram's parents facilitated this passion by setting up a well-equipped workshop within 'The Retreat'. This workshop, aligned with the Montessori method of learning, was complete with lathes, drills, a foundry, and a mechanical instructor. Eventually, a physics and chemistry laboratory was added, providing Vikram with all the necessary tools to further explore and indulge in his scientific interests. Vikram spent considerable time in this workshop, gaining hands-on experience that would later be invaluable in his scientific research.

In addition to his practical experiments, Vikram was well-versed in the works of popular science writers of the era. He kept abreast of the latest developments in physics and rocketry, likely informed by local newspapers, indicating a keen awareness of the rapidly evolving scientific landscape.

Ahmedabad, mirroring the intellectual curiosity prevalent in many Indian cities at the time, boasted a vibrant press that catered to a public highly interested in science. An example of this fervour was Pramod Kale, a physicist from Poona, who built his own radio during his school days and devoured the works of Jules Verne, serialised in a Marathi children's magazine. Educational institutions provided access to a plethora of magazines and technical journals, including notable publications like Nature, Popular Science, Popular Mechanics, and Wireless World. Vikram Sarabhai, with the resources at his disposal, undoubtedly had access to an even broader range of scientific literature, including the latest Western scientific magazines.

The field of physics was undergoing a thrilling phase of discovery and innovation during this period. The early 20th century saw the discovery of the electron, which triggered rapid advancements in atomic physics. In 1932, British scientists John Douglas Cockcroft and Ernest Thomas Sinton Walton developed a controlled method for splitting the atomic nucleus, advancing beyond the previous experiments of Ernest Rutherford and James Chadwick involving alpha particles. Meanwhile, Irene Curie and Frederic Joliot achieved breakthroughs in artificial radioactivity, and new atomic particles were being discovered regularly.

The fascination with space travel was already taking flight, despite the airplane still being a relatively recent invention. Werner Von Braun, destined to become the architect of Germany's V-2 rockets, was experimenting with missile technology in the 1920s, inspired by Hermann Oberth's seminal book The Rocket into Planetary Space. This book, rich with formulas and a detailed exploration of rocket physics, captured the imagination of many. The German filmmaker Fritz Lang even created a film titled Frau im Mond (Woman in the Moon), reflecting the era's intense interest in space exploration. In the United States, engineer Robert Goddard had launched the first liquid-fuelled rocket, and Constantin Generales, a medical student, was conducting experiments on the effects of space on mice by 1931.

These developments were likely to have fuelledVikram's passion for science. However, Vikram was not destined for a conventional scientific career. To truly appreciate the breadth of his achievements, it's crucial to recognise that his fascination was not confined to a specific field of physics or a solitary scientific question. Vikram was captivated by science as a whole—its foundations, methods, precision and objectives. In a 1966 talk, he addressed a common misconception, stating that contrary to popular belief, the pursuit of science, like philosophy, literature or art, involves imagination and intuition. He emphasised the unique quality of a scientist being his unwavering commitment to testing concepts through observation, willing to let even the most elaborate theories crumble under the weight of experimental evidence.

Vikram Sarabhai possessed a unique ability to see aestheticism in science, particularly in its pursuit of patterns. He believed that by discerning the harmony in what seemed like noise, one could find the work immensely rewarding. This perspective was a testament to his ability to blend scientific rigour with a sense of beauty. He successfully applied this scientific approach to a wide array of activities beyond the realm of pure science, including business, management studies, and market research. However, it was in the field of science that he found a profound fulfilment of his innate inclinations, which included a sense of duty, a love for beauty, and a deeply-rooted sense of patriotism.

In May 1966, at the International Symposium on Science and Society in South Asia held at Rockefeller University in New York, Vikram Sarabhai elaborated on these themes. His speech provided insight into the motivations that shaped his career and contributions. He emphasised that a person versed in scientific methods brings a new perspective and enlightenment to problem-solving, offering valuable leadership. He acknowledged the challenges faced by scientists in India, noting that working conditions and facilities often paled in comparison to those in other countries. This reality led to frustration for some and even prompted others to leave the country.

However, Sarabhai pointed out that those who could apply their scientific insights to address the problems of their community and nation discovered an exhilarating field of work. For these individuals, the effort was intrinsically rewarding, even if the results were slow to materialise. This approach to science and its application to societal issues was not just a professional choice for Sarabhai but a reflection of his deeply-held belief in the value of science for the betterment of society and the nation.

❑

The Beginning of Many Things in Life

In the serene setting of 'The Retreat's' lawns, a gathering unfolded featuring children, teachers, and parents. The focal point of this assembly was Gautam and Vikram, who were adorned with garlands, indicating a significant moment in their lives. This occasion was marked by a formal photograph, capturing the moment before these young men embarked on their educational journey abroad, following in the footsteps of their older siblings, Suhrid and Bharti, who had previously left for Oxford.

In their hometown of Ahmedabad, a city where business skills were often valued over academic achievements, not everyone chose the path of overseas education. This was exemplified by Vikram's friends, Arvind and Chinubhai Lalbhai, who remained in Ahmedabad to manage their family businesses, with Chinubhai eventually becoming the city's mayor.

Vikram's academic journey included his time at 'The Retreat' and RC High School, and later at Gujarat College. Established by the British in 1887, Gujarat College was a symbol of colonial architecture, surrounded by a dense forest and located across the Sabarmati River, connected to the city by the Ellis Bridge.

During his tenure at Gujarat College, Vikram distinguished himself in physics and chemistry, while also developing a keen interest in Sanskrit poetry. His college life was filled with activities like cycling and playing cricket for the college team. This period represented a time when Vikram closely experienced the life of an average Indian student.

The next phase of Vikram's education was at Cambridge University, secured through a letter of recommendation from family friend Rabindranath Tagore. St John's College, happy to accept him, became his new academic home.

In 1937, Vikram and Gautam embarked on their journey to England. On the same ship, they met Raj, who would later marry Khushwant Singh. An anecdote from this journey highlights the luxury they enjoyed, being able to speak daily with their father over the phone, a rarity in that era.

Vikram's social life in Cambridge was vibrant, and known for hosting memorable parties, although he and his brother refrained from drinking. His time at Cambridge, from 1937 to 1940, is well-documented in photographs that depict him in fashionable clothing, often accompanied by a large dog.

Professor SM Chitre later remarked on Vikram's fitting in seamlessly at Cambridge, suggesting that his curious nature thrived amidst the university's eclectic atmosphere, surrounded by mellow stone buildings, tree-lined avenues, and picturesque cafés.

During Vikram's tenure at Cambridge, he exhibitedminimal engagement in extra-curricular activities. The only notable association was his fellowship with the Cambridge Philosophical Society, a stark contrast to contemporaries like Indira Gandhi,

Jawaharlal Nehru's daughter, who was actively involved in political endeavours at Oxford during the same period.

Vikram's devotion to his scientific studies was intense and singular. This commitment was so profound that his sister Gita, upon visiting him, found him deeply engrossed in his work, almost to the point of being overwhelmed.

In the visual records of that era, Vikram's presence is captured as elusive and almost spectral. Film footage portrays him as a shadowy figure moving swiftly through the Cambridge shrubbery. His appearance was marked by smooth skin, sharp features, and an almost effeminate quality, balanced by a determined expression and piercing eyes. His full lips and abundant hair swept back from a wide forehead added to his distinctive persona.

However, Vikram's time at Cambridge was not during the institution's peak in physics research. The Cavendish and Mond laboratories, once celebrated for groundbreaking discoveries in physics, had lost their leading edge. This decline was in stark contrast to their achievements in the early 1930s under Ernest Rutherford's leadership, a period marked by significant scientific breakthroughs like Chadwick's discovery of the neutron and the pioneering work in electron-positron pairs by Blackett and Occhialini.

Vikram's arrival at Cambridge coincided with this period of diminished prominence in physics. The death of Ernest Rutherford, a luminary in the field and a guiding force behind the laboratories' earlier successes, symbolised the end of an era of remarkable discoveries at these institutions.

With the passing of Ernest Rutherford, a significant chapter in the history of the Cavendish and Mond laboratories at Cambridge came to a close, marking the end of a golden era in physics research. Vikram, deeply immersed in the experimental study of cosmic rays rather than atomic fission, might not have felt this loss as acutely as some of his peers. Nevertheless, he was inevitably influenced by the growing sense of desolation that enveloped the scientific community during this period. The rise of Hitler and the ensuing turmoil in Europe added to the sombre atmosphere. The exodus of Jewish scientists fleeing for their lives, many bound for America, foreshadowed a shift in the global scientific landscape, with the United States poised to become the new epicentre of scientific innovation.

In that transformative summer, revelations about the potential of Uranium-235 to cause massive explosions were rippling through the scientific world. The outbreak of World War II in September 1939 further compounded the global tension.

Back in India, Ambalal, Vikram's father, was consumed with worry for his sons' safety amid the escalating conflict. He urgently called for their return home. However, it took several months into the war before Vikram could make his journey back to India. This interruption in his academic pursuits was a significant concern for him. By then, he had completed his undergraduate studies in physics and mathematics and was contemplating his future academic endeavours. Vikram sought guidance from Cambridge regarding the continuation of his postgraduate research in India. He received the green light to proceed, provided his work was supervised by the esteemed CV Raman. Thus, in 1940, with a tripos in the natural sciences, Vikram returned to India and made his way to the Indian Institute of Science (IISc) in Bangalore.

The origins of IISc trace back to the vision of the Bombay industrialist Jamshetji Tata. In 1898, Tata announced his ambitious plan to establish an institution dedicated to the advancement of science, technology, medicine, psychology and philosophy. However, it was not until after his death in 1911 that his vision materialised, with the aim of nurturing the brightest minds to serve the nation effectively. The IISc, characterised by its colonial-style grey stone buildings amidst a lush expanse of greenery, initially focused on applied sciences with departments in chemistry and electrical engineering. By the time Vikram arrived in 1940, the institute had expanded to include a physics department, under the leadership of the renowned CV Raman.

Born in 1888 in the rural south of India, Chandrasekhara Venkata Raman embarked on a remarkable journey that would lead him to groundbreaking discoveries in physics. Initially working as a government servant, Raman dedicated his spare time to the study of physics, a pursuit driven by passion more than professional obligation. His deep investigations into the scattering of light led to the discovery of the phenomenon later known as the 'Raman Effect'. This groundbreaking discovery, which significantly advanced the understanding of light and its interactions, earned him the prestigious Nobel Prize in Physics in 1930.

Raman's physical appearance was as distinctive as his scientific contributions. He was thin and had a sallow complexion, his countenance marked by doleful eyes and further distinguished by his characteristic turban. His undeniable genius exuded a sense of certainty so profound that, as one fellow scientist remarked, Raman's brilliance would have been recognised with a Nobel Prize even in the most remote and unlikely locations, such as Antarctica.

When Vikram Sarabhai arrived at the Indian Institute of Science to work under Raman's guidance, it is believed that Raman received him warmly. The Sarabhais were a well-known family, and Raman was already acquainted with them. Ambalal, Vikram's father, had personally written to Raman, requesting him to mentor his son. Raman not only agreed to this but also played a pivotal role in steering Vikram towards his future area of research.

Vikram's research would focus on cosmic rays, mysterious and penetrating radiations emanating from outer space. The existence of cosmic rays had been initially suggested by CTR Wilson, renowned for inventing the cloud chamber in 1911. While their extra-terrestrial origin had been confirmed through high-altitude investigations by scientists like Father Wulf and Victor Hess, much about these radiations remained a mystery. Further studies by scientists like Clay and Störmer had begun to reveal how factors like latitude and longitude affected the intensity of cosmic ray radiation.

In those times, cosmic rays were a subject of significant interest, mainly due to their highly charged state. They offered a valuable resource in an era predating the development of giant accelerators, serving as a 'poor man's laboratory' for physicists. However, the specific area of Vikram's research on cosmic rays was not particularly trendy or widely explored. When Vikram was ready to submit his PhD thesis titled 'Cosmic Ray Investigations in Tropical Latitudes', Cambridge University faced the challenge of finding an oral examiner with the necessary expertise in this niche field, a testament to the novelty and specialised nature of his research.

In the context of Vikram Sarabhai's research under CV Raman, the choice of his research focus appears somewhat unconventional, considering Raman's divergent academic pursuits. By that time, Raman, a Nobel laureate renowned for his work on light scattering, had shifted his focus towards the study of sound waves. He was also engaged in amassing a collection of crystals. This shift in Raman's interests makes Vikram's selection for cosmic ray research all the more intriguing.

A plausible explanation for this divergence, as Vikram himself hints in his thesis, may be attributed to the influence of Robert Millikan's visit to India. Millikan, an esteemed American scientist who won the Nobel Prize in 1923 for his work on the electron charge, was instrumental in coining the term 'cosmic rays'. His visit to India in 1937, aimed at gathering data for his global survey of cosmic ray intensity, included a meeting with Raman. Millikan's return in 1940 for stratospheric balloon ascents further highlighted the significance of cosmic ray research.

Vikram's thesis emphasises that most cosmic ray research of that era was concentrated in temperate regions. However, South India, strategically located along the magnetic equator, presented a unique and valuable opportunity for cosmic ray studies. Millikan's visits and the potential they demonstrated might have encouraged Raman to propose the initiation of experimental research in this area at Bangalore. Vikram noted that initial plans to conduct a detailed high-altitude survey across various latitudes in India to augment Millikan's results were hampered by wartime constraints in acquiring necessary equipment like balloons and radio apparatus.

Instead of pursuing these extensive surveys, Vikram chose the Geiger counter as his primary research tool. This choice differed from Raman's suggestion, as recalled by Raman's nephew, S Ramaseshan, an established scientist himself. Raman had recommended that Vikram use photographic emulsion plates to detect cosmic rays, similar to the method used by Marietta Blau and Herta Wambacher in 1937. Raman believed that this approach might lead to a significant discovery, potentially meriting a Nobel Prize. However, Vikram preferred the Geiger counter for its precision and adaptability. In retrospect, as Ramaseshan recounts, Vikram later reflected that had he followed Raman's advice, he might have discovered a new particle like CF Powell, who later won the Nobel Prize for such a discovery using photo plates.

Vikram's initial experiments culminated in his first paper, 'The Time Distribution of Cosmic Rays', which he presented to the Indian Academy of Sciences in 1942. On this occasion,

Raman introduced Vikram with high praise, acknowledging his privileged upbringing but emphasising his dedication to original experiments. Raman expressed his strong belief in Vikram's potential to significantly contribute to the growth of science in India, a testament to the promising start of Vikram's illustrious scientific career.

The speech delivered by CV Raman introducing Vikram Sarabhai at the Indian Academy of Sciences in 1942 could be interpreted in various ways. It is unclear whether Raman's praise was a genuine reflection of his belief in Vikram's scientific capabilities, or if it was influenced by the Sarabhai family's prominent reputation. Vikram, on his part, held his mentor in high esteem. This respect was evident a few years later when Raman expressed his desire to establish his own institute, the Raman Institute. Vikram played a crucial role in this endeavour, connecting Raman with industrialists in Ahmedabad and aiding in the collection of significant capital for the project. A photograph from later years, showing the two men sitting side by side on cane chairs, engrossed in papers on a lawn, hints at a relationship marked by mutual fondness and comfort.

Another significant relationship Vikram cultivated at the Indian Institute of Science (IISc) was with Homi Bhabha, a towering figure in Indian science. Bhabha, who would later establish India's atomic energy programme, had an illustrious academic career, having attended Cambridge a decade before Vikram. He earned several fellowships, including the Isaac Newton Studentship, and collaborated with renowned scientists like Wolfgang Pauli and Enrico Fermi in Europe. Bhabha's contributions to physics, particularly his papers on positron physics and the cascade theory of cosmic showers, had already set him apart as a leading scientist.

Bhabha found himself in India during a holiday when World War II broke out. He accepted a readership offer at the IISc and used this time to further his theoretical work from Cambridge and conduct experiments on the 'hard component' of cosmic rays. While Bhabha's interest in cosmic rays primarily stemmed from the atomic particles they emitted, Vikram viewed them as a means to explore outer space.

The coming together of Vikram and Bhabha at the IISc was a serendipitous event, marking the beginning of a professional relationship that would significantly influence India's technological development. Despite their different approaches, they shared intriguing similarities and developed a deep professional rapport.

Beyond their professional alignment, Vikram and Bhabha shared several commonalities. Both came from affluent backgrounds: Bhabha was related to the Tata family, a prominent industrial group in Bombay, while Vikram hailed from the wealthy Sarabhai family in western India. This was unusual for the time, as most scientists then typically came from the southern or eastern parts of India. Both men were also noted for their sophistication, with Bhabha being more Westernised in his demeanour. They were also known for their distinct appearances: Bhabha with his dark, intense look, and Vikram with his delicate features, adding to the facets that drew them together in Bangalore.

Vikram Sarabhai, known for his scientific acumen, was also notable for his strikingly translucent complexion, described evocatively by S Ramaseshan as resembling a baby's skin with an underlying flow of milk. Beyond his scientific endeavours, Vikram, along with Homi Bhabha, indulged in a lifestyle rich with cultural and intellectual pursuits. Their evenings were often spent at the upscale West End Hotel, mingling with a circle of local intellectuals and friends, including the charming Sri Lankan woman, Anil D'Silva. These social gatherings, perceived as playboy-type activities, contrasted sharply with the more conservative lifestyle of their middle-class Tamil Brahmin peers, who viewed Vikram and Bhabha with a mix of scandal and envy.

Vikram's affluent background afforded him a lifestyle far removed from the typical student experience. Eschewing the confined spaces of student hostels, he chose to reside in a house with a picturesque view located in Malleswaram, a leafy suburb in the northern part of the city. This house, named 'Premalaya', was rumoured to have once been the residence of the veteran Congress leader S Nijalingappa. In 'Premalaya', with its stone floors and distinctively angled rooms, Vikram established his personal space, under the attentive care of his devoted assistant, Lala Inkayya.

In moments of solitude, Vikram often found himself drawn to the Vedanta College, run by the Ramakrishna Mission. There, he engaged in profound discussions on Hindu philosophy with the resident priests. These philosophical explorations deeply influenced Vikram, as he later revealed in a 1962 public lecture. He spoke of how ancient Indian philosophers' understanding of knowledge, the observer's role, and the concept of relativity had struck him. Vikram posited that the remarkable progress of modern physics could be attributed to its recognition of these very concepts and the development of a mathematical framework to quantitatively express them. This blend of scientific inquiry and philosophical introspection defined a significant aspect of Vikram Sarabhai's multifaceted persona.

In Bangalore, Vikram Sarabhai dedicated himself tirelessly to his research. His work ethic and approach caught the attention of Bruno Rossi, a luminary in X-ray astronomy and space plasma physics at the Massachusetts Institute of Technology (MIT). Rossi, with whom Vikram would later collaborate annually, admired Vikram's extraordinary ability to assimilate a vast array of experimental and theoretical data. Rossi believed that Vikram possessed what he described as 'an almost uncanny capability to absorb and store in his mind a vast amount of experimental and theoretical data'. Vikram's method involved not just data accumulation but also an artistically intuitive process of organising this information into a coherent and evolving picture, revealing previously unseen regularities and relationships. For Vikram, Rossi noted, scientific research was much more than a profession; it was an act of love towards nature.

Scientific research remained Vikram's enduring passion, a constant source of fulfilment amidst his busy life. However, his legacy extended beyond his scientific endeavours. Unlike Homi Bhabha, who gained early distinction as a scientist, Vikram's fame was not anchored in his scientific discoveries but in his ability to establish institutions and actualise ideas aligned with a deeply humane vision. His time at the Vedanta College in Bangalore was not solely dedicated to science; it also involved significant personal and philosophical development. Like his father Ambalal, Vikram was introspective about life and selfhood. However, his reflections were more action-oriented than his father's. He advised his friend and fellow scientist MGK Menon, emphasising the ability to leap and run in life rather than taking cautious steps. He spoke of initiating processes with the confidence and precision of a prophet. This self-assured approach, evident in his later endeavours, likely took shape during his student days in Bangalore.

Vikram's innovative ideas were reflected in his talks and papers in later life. For instance, in a paper presented in October 1969, he discussed the ecological balance in the context of living organisms and their environment, drawing parallels with Mahatma Gandhi's principles in the social context. He talked about merging responsibilities with rights, an idea that resonated with Gandhian philosophy.

In a 1965 broadcast on All India Radio about 'Leadership in Science', Vikram expounded on his management philosophy, which applied to both companies and large institutions. He emphasised a non-hierarchical approach, viewing a leader more as a cultivator providing the right environment for growth rather than a conventional manufacturer.

Vikram's time in Bangalore was a period of intellectual incubation and exploration. It was a phase where he was actively scouting ideas, forming alliances, and laying the groundwork for future projects. This period was also the most hedonistic phase of his life. Influenced by the Jain principles of self-reflection and Maria Montessori's emphasis on sensory experiences, Vikram adeptly balanced hard work with sensual pleasures. During his student years in Bangalore, he indulged in these pleasures more freely, a luxury he would forego to some extent in later years as his life became more structured.

One of Vikram's lifelong indulgences was his love for the performing arts, particularly music. Kirit Parikh, a colleague at the Department of Atomic Energy, recalled a conversation where Vikram, upon hearing Parikh's plans for an overseas trip, spontaneously suggested investing in a high-quality hi-fi system instead, highlighting Vikram's appreciation for the finer aspects of life.

This fervour led him to the musical gatherings, or kutcheris, in southern India, where he quickly became a recognised figure. In this close-knit community of music aficionados, his striking looks and charisma didn't go unnoticed. He formed friendships with many local artists, including the legendary MS Subbulakshmi, who would later grace one of his conferences with her performance.

Bhabha, a man whose preferences leaned more towards symphonies and ballet, had a deep appreciation for various performing arts. He and his colleague Vikram eventually decided to organise a dance event to support a charitable cause. Vikram reached out to the renowned Bharatanatyam dancer, Ram Gopal, for assistance. This venture led to Vikram's encounter with Mrinalini Swaminathan.

Their paths had crossed before. The Swaminathans were a prominent family in southern India. Mrinalini's father,

Swaminathan, was a distinguished lawyer at the Madras High Court and a proponent of progressive ideas. He had encouraged his wife, Ammu, to embrace a sophisticated and modern lifestyle, a stance she maintained even after his demise. This was a bold decision in an era where widows often faced social ostracism. Ammu had also ventured into politics, during which she met Sarla Sarabhai. The two shared many similarities; for instance, Ammu's elder daughter, Lakshmi, paralleled Mridula in her idealistic fervour. Lakshmi would gain fame as Captain Lakshmi Sehgal of Subhash Chandra Bose's Indian National Army, a volunteer force aimed at liberating India through armed struggle.

Mrinalini, unlike her sister, charted a different path. Vikram first met her when the Sarabhais were in Madras, en route to the hill station Ooty. Dressed in tennis shorts, she epitomised the emerging socialite. Vikram's initial invitation to a movie seemed casual, and he later admitted to being somewhat put off by her seemingly frivolous demeanour. However, their subsequent meeting in Bangalore revealed a profound change in her. The once carefree teenager had transformed into a sophisticated and elegant young woman, far removed from the frivolous image he remembered. Mrinalini had taken a significant turn in her life, immersing herself deeply in the study of Bharatanatyam. This journey took her from Tagore's Santiniketan to Ram Gopal's dance school in Bangalore. She even vowed to remain unmarried, dedicating herself entirely to her art. Her commitment, mirroring Vikram's own dedication to science, resonated with him. He asked her out, and they began dating, exploring a new chapter in their lives together.

Vikram and Mrinalini's romance blossomed with long, idyllic drives in Vikram's Bantham and endless, deep conversations. They savoured fresh makkai (corn) and shared a love for poetry, with Mrinalini reciting Bengali verses reminiscent of Tagore and Santiniketan, while Vikram recited lines from Kalidasa. Despite their repeated disinterest in marriage, their relationship grew steadily closer. In her autobiography, Mrinalini reflects on this period.

She was captivated by Vikram's intellectual prowess and maturity beyond his years. His vision and breadth of knowledge were astounding. They shared a myriad of common interests: a love for beauty, honesty, tradition and their country, coupled with an excitement for new developments in civilisation. Mrinalini noted the similarities between science and art, both recognising the holistic nature of the cosmos. Their shared experiences, Vikram as a scientist and she as a dancer, created a unique bond, a 'togetherness' that was difficult to articulate. Vikram's affection for her was evident, more through his actions than words.

Vikram's family also noticed changes in him. Gita, Vikram's sister, recalled a holiday in the South when they impulsively climbed a hill, which worried their mother, Sarla. This youthful behaviour highlighted Vikram's evolving character. He became more affectionate, complimenting his sisters on their appearances, and sharing books with them about womanhood. He began to seek advice from his sisters, particularly about Mrinalini, even asking Gita to select a sari for her, signalling a significant shift in his behaviour.

Vikram was a passionate lover, according to Vinodini Mayor, Mrinalini's cousin. Post their wedding, Vinodini observed that Vikram was deeply in love, his attention solely focused on Mrinalini. When Mrinalini went to Madras for training, Vikram maintained constant communication, calling her every night and visiting every weekend. His courtship style was unique and unconventional. Mrinalini humorously recalled that she never received a traditional gift from him. For their engagement, Vikram, despite his wealth, chose a simple yet meaningful turquoise Tibetan ring. In another instance, he sent her a dark-eyed slender loris, a gift she adamantly refused to accept.

Vikram's relentless pursuit of Mrinalini was notable for several reasons. Firstly, although Mrinalini acknowledged her love for him, she remained uncertain about her feelings. Her concerns revolved around cultural differences between the north and the south of India, and the impact of marriage, particularly since Vikram had proposed, on her dancing career. Secondly, Vikram faced subtle opposition from his family. Despite their close-knit nature, the Sarabhais expressed reservations about Mrinalini. Vikram introduced her to his family, including a dinner with his brother Suhrid and his wife Manorama in Bangalore, and a picnic with his parents in Mahabalipuram.

Vikram's father, Ambalal, wrote a letter voicing his concerns about Mrinalini being young, inexperienced and ambitious, and urged Vikram to make a careful decision. While it's unclear how Vikram reacted to this lukewarm assessment, he remained undeterred in his commitment to Mrinalini. Eventually, with support from her family, Mrinalini consented to the marriage.

Vikram's urgency to marry at a young age, despite these hurdles, might seem perplexing. However, understanding the context of the times is crucial. Earlier that year, the Stafford Cripps mission had failed to secure the Indian National Congress's support for the British war effort in exchange for dominion status. Congress, instead, at a meeting in Gandhi's Sevagram Ashram in July 1942, demanded that the British 'quit' India. This period was marked by political turmoil and personal crises within the Sarabhai household, intensifying the sense of urgency. Ambalal, worried about the tumultuous times, urged Vikram to return home.

On 8 August 1942, the Quit India resolution, moved by Jawaharlal Nehru, was passed at the historic Gowalia Tank meeting in Bombay, with Gandhi's rallying cry of 'Do or die!' Nehru referred to it as the 'zero hour of the world'. Amidst growing pressure from his family in Ahmedabad, Vikram's desire to marry intensified. Mrinalini speculated that Vikram feared they might be separated permanently, leading to a loss of their relationship. This anxiety, possibly fuelled by the chaotic atmosphere of the era or his deep affection for Mrinalini, spurred Vikram's persistence. Ultimately, his determination prevailed, and their wedding was scheduled for the last week of August 1942.

Their wedding had to be a modest affair. Mrinalini's sister, Lakshmi, was incarcerated in Singapore alongside other members of the Indian National Army, and due to disrupted rail connections, none of Vikram's family could attend. The only representative from Vikram's side was his majordomo, Lala. In such circumstances, one might expect a young man like Vikram to be nervous, but his concern seemed primarily focused on his bride-to-be. On the wedding morning, he sought out blue lotuses in the bazaar, arranged them on a brass tray, and sent them to Mrinalini's room. This thoughtful gesture deeply touched her, dissolving any lingering hesitations she had.

The ceremony, a blend of simple Vedic rituals followed by a civil service, was held in the Swaminathan family drawing room. Mrinalini chose a white khadi sari and adorned herself with flowers instead of traditional jewellery. Her thali, a symbol of marital commitment, was a Lakshmi pendant Vikram had purchased in Bangalore. A musician friend serenaded the gathering with the veena. In a unique touch, at Vikram's request, Mrinalini and a dancer friend performed a scene from the Ramayana depicting a deer. They embarked for Ahmedabad that night.

Their journey was through a tumultuous landscape. Following the Quit India movement, the nation was in turmoil, with widespread strikes and protests. Communications were severed, and infrastructure was damaged. As Katherine Frank noted, India appeared on the brink of insurrection and anarchy. The trip to Bombay, where they were to catch a train to Ahmedabad, was fraught with delays due to sabotaged railway tracks, turning their journey into an unconventional 60-hour honeymoon in a first-class coupe.

Upon arrival, they were met with a sombre atmosphere at 'The Retreat', Vikram's family home. Four of his sisters and two aunts were imprisoned; Mridula was serving an eighteen-month sentence. More distressing was the illness of Suhrid, the eldest Sarabhai sibling, believed to have been contracted during a business trip to Africa. Ambalal appealed for his daughters' release to visit their sick brother, a request partially granted by the governor, Sir Roger Lumley. However, Mridula declined parole.

The family faced these challenges for several months. While Vikram undoubtedly shared his family's concern for Suhrid's health, he displayed a remarkable ability to maintain focus on his long-term goals amidst personal and external crises. This trait, which could be interpreted as either extreme dedication or a lack of ordinary emotion, led him to continue his scientific research even as personal and national turmoil swirled around him.

Vikram's scientific journey led him to Poona, where he sought assistance in constructing a complex set of Geiger counters for his experiments. He approached the Poona Observatory, part of the India Meteorological Department (IMD), one of the few institutions in the country with the necessary expertise. The Deputy Director General of the IMD, Dr KR Ramanathan, welcomed Vikram and his wife with gracious hospitality.

It's plausible that the connection was facilitated by Sir CV Raman, under whom Ramanathan had studied. This meeting was not only productive in addressing Vikram's immediate needs, as he later moved his equipment to the IMD's research laboratory to leverage its more accurate meteorological data, but it also had significant long-term implications. Ramanathan, an expert in aeronomy and atmospheric physics, would become an integral part of the broader research project Vikram envisioned.

In 1943, Vikram embarked on a trip to Kashmir to conduct high-altitude studies of cosmic rays. Such studies are valuable because cosmic ray intensity increases significantly with elevation, and higher altitudes allow for the investigation of types of radiation that do not survive to sea level. In his PhD thesis, Vikram noted his preference for an altitude above 14,100 feet—the altitude at which similar studies were conducted at St Evans in America—but due to the lack of facilities at such heights in India, he settled for a lower altitude in Kashmir. This choice, however, came with its own set of logistical challenges, which he detailed in his thesis. These descriptions also highlight the advantages Vikram had in terms of wealth and family support, which played a significant role in facilitating his research endeavours.

The selection of the expedition site, Gangabal, was finalised after Vikram arrived in Srinagar and following consultations with experienced trekkers, including Major Huddow, a participant in the recent Nanga Parbat expedition. The governor of Kashmir not only offered advice but also arranged for the transportation of forty pack ponies and fifty porters.

The group departing Srinagar on 3 September comprised Vikram, Mrinalini, his siblings Gira and Gautam, a laboratory assistant from Bangalore, a camp manager, Dr Dayal Singh of the Kashmir Medical Service, the transport manager Pandit Tikkalal, four personal servants, three helpers, a khansamah (cook) with tents, furniture and provisions from a trekking agency, and a state-provided guard. The total entourage, including each individual's riding pony, amounted to ninety people.

The trek to the site was challenging, with steep and sometimes vanishing paths, requiring the travellers to leap from one boulder to another. Vikram meticulously recorded these difficulties alongside more pleasant experiences, such as the stunning ruins of an ancient stone temple at Nora Nag where they camped for a night.

Trunkhal was chosen for the initial cosmic ray measurements, where the team camped for four days to conduct experiments. Meanwhile, Gautam and Pandit Tikkalal scouted the vicinity of Gangabal Lake for the next observation point. They identified a suitable spot at 13,900 feet on a slope north of Gangabal. After returning to Srinagar, the expedition moved to Gulmarg, where they stayed in Nedou's Hotel. Vikram continued his observations in Gulmarg and later at Al Pathri, a short horseback ride away.

The expedition, aside from an equipment malfunction at Al Pathri, proceeded smoothly, showcasing Vikram's early managerial skills. Scientifically, the trip was successful. Vikram utilised 8mm Kodachrome cine film for his studies and concluded that the expedition had provided valuable experience in conducting high-altitude cosmic ray experiments.

As Vikram advanced in his scientific endeavours, domestic challenges began to emerge. Despite his marriage, the traditional reserve of his parents, Ambalal and Sarla, remained unchanged. Ambalal, though outwardly supportive, particularly of his daughter-in-law, would dutifully attend Mrinalini's performances, enduring the discomforts of the Town Hall rehearsals, even resorting to using an umbrella to shield himself from pigeon droppings. However, neither he nor Sarla significantly altered their behaviour to make Mrinalini feel more welcome in the family. Sarla's initial reaction to Mrinalini was particularly disheartening; she expressed surprise at her son's marriage, having always assumed he would stay a bachelor, a sentiment that did little to ease Mrinalini's sense of unease.

Meanwhile, Suhrid's health continued to deteriorate despite being moved to Bombay for better medical care.

The situation took a turn for the worse unexpectedly. While Mrinalini and Vikram were outside observing a procession, a burning canister was hurled through the air, striking Mrinalini in the eye. The days following the incident were fraught with tension and uncertainty about the possibility of her losing vision in that eye. The treatment process was prolonged and fraught with anxiety. During this challenging period, Vikram was a constant presence by Mrinalini's side. According to Mrinalini's biographer, Harriet Ronken Lynton, Vikram was unwavering in his support, never leaving her bedside. This dedication was further echoed by Vinodini, who recalled the daily telegrams sent by Vikram to their home in Kerala, where Mrinalini went to receive Ayurvedic treatment. He even followed these messages by visiting in person. During this time of recovery, they received the sorrowful news of Suhrid's passing.

In the aftermath of these events, Vikram decided to leave the increasingly gloomy environment of 'The Retreat', his family home. The loss of their eldest son was a profound blow to Ambalal and Sarla, leaving a lasting melancholic imprint; even twenty years later, Erik Erikson noted a sombre atmosphere around Ambalal. Vikram, seeking a fresh start, returned to the Indian Institute of Science (IISc) in Bangalore. The house on the hillock in Malleswaram, which they called 'Premalaya', meaning 'abode of love', was reopened and prepared for their return. This time, the house truly lived up to its name, as Vikram returned with his beloved wife, Mrinalini, to start a new chapter in their lives together.

Their return to Bangalore stirred a wave of excitement in the otherwise tranquil garden city. Vikram, with his strikingly handsome appearance, twinkling eyes, and undeniable charm, had always been a charismatic figure. Many shared Mrinalini's initial impression of him resembling a prince. Mrinalini, while not fitting the conventional standards of beauty, compensated with her attractive features, elegant poise, and refined taste. Together, they were the epitome of an ideal couple, possessing good looks, wealth and success, and they had daringly bridged cultural and geographical divides in the name of love. Their relationship seemed like something out of a fairy tale, captivating even schoolgirls in Bangalore who would sneak out to the quiet suburb just for a chance to see the illustrious couple drive by.

However, the actuality of their life was far less glamorous. Upon their return, Vikram immersed himself in his work with an almost obsessive dedication. He had previously been engaged in studying the time distribution of cosmic rays and planning his expedition to Kashmir. During this period, following a suggestion from Bhabha, Vikram devised a 'direct method' for measuring the intensity of slow mesons using the Geiger counter.

Slow mesons, particles generated by the collision of primary radiation with atoms in the upper atmosphere, are typically found only near their point of origin. Vikram had observed slight variations in their intensity day-to-day and at different hours, a discovery that prompted him to veer from his initial research and delve into a new study on the temporal fluctuations of cosmic rays.

His dedication saw him spending extended periods, often including nights, confined within the plain walls of the laboratory. Mrinalini, growing weary of waiting for him at home, would occasionally visit, only to fall asleep on a foldable cot in the lab. She would be awakened by Vikram in the early hours and sent home before their colleague Raman arrived. Vikram was fervently working to complete the research that would constitute the first part of his PhD thesis. During this intense period, he also managed to produce a significant paper titled 'The Method of Shower Anti-coincidences for Measuring the Meson Component of Cosmic Radiation'.

While Vikram immersed himself in his scientific pursuits, Mrinalini faced her own set of challenges. The accident that nearly cost her an eye had weakened her physically and left her susceptible to bouts of despondency. In a gesture of support,

Vikram encouraged her to return to dancing, an activity that was not typically pursued professionally by women at that time, and even less so by married women. His progressive stance on her career was noteworthy, especially considering the prevailing societal norms. To facilitate her practice, Vikram had an additional floor constructed at 'Premalaya' and proposed inviting a dance teacher to reside with them. He also took an active role in her performances, accompanying her to shows in various locations, overseeing production aspects, and even managing the stage lighting himself.

In the following year, with the end of World War II, Vikram began planning his return to Cambridge to pursue his doctorate. Conscious of the setbacks Mrinalini had faced due to her injury, he suggested she remain in India to continue her dance career. However, Mrinalini, not wanting to be apart from him, declined the offer. Consequently, in 1945, they embarked on a strenuous journey to England via a Dakota aircraft, marking the beginning of a new chapter in their lives as Mr and Mrs Vikram Sarabhai.

Upon arrival, they encountered a Britain still reeling from the war's devastation. The landscape was scarred with bombed-out buildings and the populace was grappling with rationing. Cambridge University, renowned for its scientific community, had been significantly impacted by the war, losing many of its scientists. Post-war, students whose studies had been interrupted were returning in large numbers. However, there was a notable void in leadership, especially in the nuclear physics department, which had once been illustrious. Joan Freeman, an Australian-born scientist who arrived at the Cavendish Laboratory in 1946, initially experienced disappointment at the state of the university.

Yet, there were still glimmers of inspiration at Cambridge. Freeman marvelled at the 50-foot tall, high-voltage machines developed following the historic 1932 experiment by Cockcroft and Walton, the ethereal singing of choir boys in King's College

Chapel, and the serene activity of punting on the Cam. The university still hosted eminent figures like Paul Adrian Maurice Dirac, delivering lectures on mathematics. Other notable personalities present at the time included George Lindsay, future chief of the Canadian Department of National Defence's Operational Research Establishment, Charles Barnes, who would later become a senior professor at the California Institute of Technology, Godfrey Stafford, future director of the Rutherford Laboratory, and Allan Cormack, destined to win the Nobel Prize in Medicine in 1979. Freeman was part of a diverse group of 'colonials', a term for overseas students that included Canadians, South Africans and Australians, but notably no Indians. She also observed the activities of the Cambridge Interplanetary Society, which was engaged in theoretical research on space propulsion. Despite society's ambitious goals, such space endeavours were considered impractical at the time and not taken seriously.

During Vikram's academic tenure, there is no record of him being directly involved with the thriving scientific activities mentioned earlier. According to Mrinalini, Vikram was working intensely during this period. His PhD thesis introduction reveals he focused on two primary areas: interpreting data on cosmic ray intensity variations collected in India and experimenting with high-energy gamma rays to measure photofission cross-section.

Vikram's thesis credits suggest much of his work was self-initiated, which seems plausible given that his research area was somewhat peripheral to Cambridge's main scientific interests at the time. For his cosmic ray intensity variation studies, he acknowledges collaborating with Dr P Nicholson at the Cavendish Laboratory but emphasises that he independently determined the scope and designed the necessary apparatus. He describes his investigations as 'entirely original' and conducted individually.

In the second area of research, he credits DrWE Burcham for the idea of accurately determining the photofission cross-section and for periodic valuable advice. However, Vikram clarifies that the entire experiment was his own effort, including an innovative method for measuring X-ray flux. He expresses gratitude to CV Raman for continuous encouragement and supervision of his work in India and to Bhabha for discussions about cosmic rays. Additionally, he acknowledges ES Shire for supervising his research at Cambridge and thanks various colleagues, particularly Dr WE Burcham, Mr DRL Wilkinson and MrEB Paul, for their assistance.

Vikram also co-authored two papers with P Nicholson: 'The Semi-diurnal Variation in Meson Intensity' presented at the Physical Society Cambridge Conference in 1947, and 'The Semi-diurnal Variation in Cosmic Ray Intensity' published in the Proceedings of the Physical Society in 1948.

Vikram's extensive lab work, however, took a toll on his health, leading to a malaria diagnosis. The couple, residing in a single room in a boarding house, struggled with post-war Britain's fuel and food shortages, challenges exacerbated for vegetarians. Their situation was somewhat alleviated by Miss Williams, a governess who had previously worked with the Sarabhais and who came to assist them. That winter, one of the worst in a century, saw severe disruptions in coal transportation and consequent power restrictions across Britain.

Despite these challenges, this period was a happy one for Vikram and Mrinalini, perhaps their most contented time together. Freed from his family's imposing presence, Mrinalini felt liberated, and her post-accident despondency seemed to fade. She even assisted Vikram with his thesis proofs, sharing light-hearted moments of laughter and togetherness.

With the arrival of spring in March, the harsh winter gave way to a vibrant outburst of colours, with flowers transforming the landscape. Vikram completed his dissertation and travelled to Manchester for his oral examination with PMS Blackett, a renowned scientist soon to win the Nobel Prize. The examination was successful, and Vikram's PhD was recommended by Blackett and his colleague. Following the examination, Vikram and Mrinalini, who had accompanied him, toured the physics laboratory, where Blackett vividly remembered the striking contrast of Mrinalini's red sari against the lab's dull setting.

Vikram was awarded his PhD, and around the same time, Mrinalini discovered she was pregnant. They decided to embark on a celebratory European tour before returning home. In London, they purchased shoes for Vikram's niece, Kalpana, only to receive the tragic news of her sudden passing the next day. Vikram wrote to his sister Leena, expressing his heartfelt emotions over the loss.

Despite this sadness, the couple enjoyed their holiday, exploring European theatres as Vikram planned to build one for Mrinalini's performances in Ahmedabad. They indulged in café dining, street roaming, and reconnecting with acquaintances, returning home in 1947 with a plethora of exciting plans and hopes.

On 15 August 1947, India achieved its long-awaited independence. Along with millions of other Indians, the Sarabhais listened intently to Prime Minister Jawaharlal Nehru's historic speech, marking the beginning of a new era of striving and service for the newly liberated nation.

❑

Shaping the Independent India

Mahatma Gandhi's inspirational words once ignited a revolutionary spirit among the Indian populace, spurring them to rise against foreign domination. In the era following India's independence, Prime Minister Jawaharlal Nehru's impassioned appeals for national service resonated deeply across a nation thirsty for progress and unity. India, at this nascent stage, was grappling with the traumatic scars left by the Partition—a bloody division that hinted at the complex challenges ahead. The fledgling nation faced a multitude of daunting tasks: fostering unity, ensuring security, alleviating poverty, and addressing the delicate issues of religion and language. Yet, there was an overwhelming willingness among the people to undertake these tasks. Chester Bowles, the American ambassador to India during the 1950s, observed this fervent spirit, particularly among the youth. He noted their explosive enthusiasm and radicalism that he interpreted as their readiness to embark on the significant democratic endeavour of nation-building.

Nehru emerged as a pivotal figure in this transformative era. While Gandhi, with his simple attire and staff, had united diverse Indian communities and instilled a moral compass in the independence movement, post-independence India craved a different form of representation. This new phase required a more assertive identity, resonating with the aspirations of a nation striving for its place in an unequal global arena. Nehru, with his aristocratic demeanour, adeptly voiced this need, which resonated throughout Asia, for a distinct, indigenous path forward. His approach was unique—he articulated these aspirations in the very language and accent of the former colonial rulers. In his initial meeting with Nehru, Bowles was struck by the Indian prime minister's dedication to Western democratic ideals, coupled with his steadfast commitment to Asian autonomy and independent thought. This sentiment, as Bowles observed across Asia, from Lebanon to Japan, was rarely expressed as eloquently as by Nehru.

Nehru was more than a symbol of national pride; he was a proponent of active citizen participation in shaping the nation's future. Speaking to Margaret Bourke-White, a photographer for the American magazine Life, Nehru emphasised the need for introspection and action in the new, free India. This sentiment resonated nationwide. Influential figures like JRD Tata and Raj Thapar echoed these views, recognising the unique opportunity to contribute to India's development during these transformative times.

This blend of assertiveness and idealism was especially evident in India's scientific community. Before independence, it was common for Indian scientists to focus their research on highlighting unique aspects of the country's conditions. For instance, Vikram Sarabhai studied cosmic rays at tropical latitudes, Homi J Bhabha conducted experiments in one of the world's deepest mineshafts in Kolar, and CV Raman utilised India's abundant sunshine to research light scattering. According to social historian Itty Abraham, these practices symbolised the integration of scientific endeavour with political aspirations.

Some scientists were driven by personal experiences. Meghnad Saha, a Bengali physicist renowned for his theory of thermal ionisation, grew up trekking ten kilometres to school through flood-prone areas, which later influenced his focus on harnessing river power. Raman, speaking at the Asian Relations Conference in 1947, emphasised the transformative potential of scientific research in addressing fundamental human challenges like hunger, poverty and disease.

Nehru's belief in the power of science was profound. He viewed science as a critical instrument in India's revolutionary transformation. During his last imprisonment before independence, he identified three key elements for India's development: a robust heavy engineering and machinery industry, scientific research institutions, and widespread electric power generation. Nehru's prioritisation of science was apparent immediately upon taking office. Amidst ongoing riots, he still made time to attend a meeting of the Council of Scientific and Industrial Research (CSIR), underscoring his belief in science as a solution to India's challenges. He consistently increased government funding for scientific research, urging scientists to focus not only on their individual quests for truth but also on the broader goal of improving the lives of India's vast population.

The establishment of the first Indian Institute of Technology in 1951 marked a significant milestone in India's post-independence scientific and educational advancement. This was followed by the creation of a network of national laboratories across the country, each specialising in various fields of research. Prime Minister Jawaharlal Nehru, reflecting on these developments in a letter to his former fellow prisoner Mahavir Tyagi in 1952, expressed pride in the establishment of these institutions. He believed that even if these were the sole achievements of the past five years, they were substantial enough to warrant recognition and commendation.

The period also witnessed a concerted effort to bolster heavy industries through comprehensive five-year plans. These plans were aimed at addressing critical national issues such as illiteracy, health care, and land reforms. Among the many priorities that Nehru had set for the nation, the challenge of energy supply remained a crucial concern. It was at this juncture that a prominent scientist, greatly admired by Nehru, stepped forward with a solution. This scientist was Homi Bhabha, a friend of physicist Vikram Sarabhai and a significant figure in Indian science. Bhabha, who chose to remain in India after the war to establish an institute of fundamental research financed by the Tata group, was admired for his patriotic decision to forego a potentially illustrious career abroad. His close relationship with Nehru catapulted him to a position of considerable influence in the realm of Indian science.

The rapid ascent of Bhabha under Nehru's patronage has been a subject of much speculation and analysis. Their shared appreciation for science and aesthetics is thought to have played a role in their unique bond. Nehru, a solitary figure amidst politicians who did not share his cultural interests, found an intellectual kinship in Bhabha. His own modest educational background possibly made him more receptive to Bhabha's intellectual prowess. S Gopal, Nehru's biographer, notes that Bhabha was among the few who addressed Nehru as 'bhai', reflecting a close personal connection. Bhabha successfully convinced Nehru of the potential of nuclear energy for power generation, a concept still in its nascent stages in the Western world at that time.

Meanwhile, Ahmedabad, the city associated with Mahatma Gandhi and Sardar Patel, India's deputy prime minister, was experiencing its own transformation in the wake of the British departure. Despite its historical resilience and adherence to traditional values, the city was not immune to the changes sweeping the nation. Ahmedabad's long-standing tradition of social responsibility, embodied in the roles of mahajan (great one) and nagarsheth (city representative), played a significant role in its response to these changes. The term 'mahajan' in Ahmedabad had several meanings, ranging from a wealthy individual to a member of the city's professional guilds, and was also associated with the cultural expectation that the affluent should contribute to the welfare of the broader community.

The nagarsheth, a position likely introduced by the Mughals, served as the city's representative and performed various public duties, including mediation between guilds and royal officials. Over time, the role of the nagarsheth evolved, with its importance shifting from hereditary lineage to social standing. For instance, the position transitioned from trading to textile families as the latter gained prominence in the city's economy.

This tradition of benevolent feudalism in Ahmedabad had long established the notion that the city's well-being was a personal responsibility of the wealthy. They often intervened during riots or epidemics, opening hospitals and providing aid. However, these acts of generosity were sometimes motivated by self-interest. For example, in the 1930s, mill owners, anticipating future labour needs, established educational institutions across various disciplines on acquired land. This foresight reflected a blend of duty and practicality, creating a rare unity among business competitors. This collaborative spirit among the city's elite was likened to a 'thick stick', symbolising their collective strength and resilience.

In the late 1940s, a period marked by India's emergence from colonial rule, a notable figure in the city of Ahmedabad was Kasturbhai Lalbhai. Despite coming from a respected nagarsheth family, Kasturbhai inherited one of the less prominent mills in the city. His physical appearance was unremarkable; he was known for his coarse features, buck teeth, and traditional dhoti attire. His blunt speech and frugal nature further distinguished him. Yet, against these seemingly modest attributes, Kasturbhai rose to prominence both locally and nationally as a leader of considerable influence. In the 1930s, he bravely challenged the powerful Tata conglomerate in a taxation dispute that had wider nationalist connotations. Despite his own relatively limited financial resources, Kasturbhai was sought after to serve on various boards and advisory committees in the newly independent India, a testament to his commitment to philanthropy and his unwavering principles.

Kasturbhai was renowned for his meticulous attention to financial ethics. His integrity was exemplified by an incident where he returned a single rupee overpayment from the Ministry of Commerce, which he had received for train fare to Delhi for a committee meeting. He even pursued legal action against a family member for embezzlement, demonstrating his unyielding commitment to honesty. Renowned advocate Nani Palkhivala remarked on Kasturbhai's unique character, highlighting his reluctance to spend on luxuries like expensive paper or envelopes, yet his willingness to donate substantial sums for educational causes, reflecting his role as not just a business leader but a nation-builder.

The foundation of Kasturbhai's significant public career can be traced back to his friendship with Ambalal, formed during the great textile strike of 1918. Ambalal, recognising Kasturbhai's negotiation skills, invited him to join the managing committee of the AMA, thus kickstarting his journey in public service. Their bond deepened when they became neighbours in Shahibaug, despite occasional strains due to business competition. Interestingly, Kasturbhai developed a special fondness for Vikram, Ambalal's son, a relationship that grew into mutual respect and affection as Vikram matured.

The connection between Vikram and Kasturbhai is noteworthy, particularly considering Vikram's own strong paternal figure. The relationship was characterised by deep mutual affection, as evidenced by Kasturbhai's emotional speeches and joint ventures. Kasturbhai's biographer, Dwijendra Tripathi, recalls an instance where Kasturbhai, while introducing Vikram at a convention, delivered a speech longer than the main speaker's. Mrinalini, Vikram's wife, recounted an episode where she was left alone while Vikram and Kasturbhai were deeply engrossed in a philosophical discussion during a visit to Mount Abu.

Kasturbhai's forthrightness and ethical values resonated with the ideals instilled in Vikram from a young age. Vikram often sought Kasturbhai's advice, valuing his experience and perspective. Moreover, Vikram's strategy to achieve his objectives often involved forming alliances, a technique he employed skillfully. He collaborated with government agencies, funding institutions, universities, and like-minded individuals, engaging in joint ventures with experienced and seasoned professionals. Kasturbhai, with his experience and wisdom, was an integral part of this network, contributing significantly to Vikram's endeavours.

Padmanabh Joshi, who completed his PhD thesis titled 'Vikram Sarabhai: A Study on Innovative Leadership and Institution Building' from Gujarat University in 1986, held a belief that Vikram Sarabhai deliberately moderated his own prominence to leverage the advantages of collaboration. His partnerships were strategic, involving individuals who brought essential skills and influence to the table. Among these were KR Ramanathan, a respected figure in scientific circles, SBhatnagar, the directorgeneral of CSIR, and Dr KS Krishnan, the director of the National Physical Laboratory (NPL), all of whom were on the board of the Physical Research Laboratory (PRL). Kasturbhai Lalbhai was another key ally, whose proximity to Nehru and other attributes were invaluable.

Ashis Nandy, a noted social theorist and critic, observed that Vikram displayed no insecurity in collaborating with individuals he deemed brighter than himself. These early partnerships set the stage for Vikram's later advocacy of interdependence, a theme he would emphasise in various forums. The synergy of Kasturbhai's entrepreneurial skills and Vikram's creativity and industriousness not only led to the creation of influential institutions but also transformed the architectural landscape of Ahmedabad. One such venture was the Ahmedabad Textile Industry's Research Association (ATIRA), envisioned after the Industrial Research Planning Committee, led by Sir RK Shanmugham Chetty, was established by the colonial government in 1944 to promote industrial research.

ATIRA was conceptualised to emulate British research associations, marking a pioneering step in Indian industrial research. It was unique in being the first cooperative venture between government and industry for research purposes and laid the groundwork for similar institutions across India. The need for such an initiative was evident, considering Ahmedabad's reliance on Manchester for technical expertise, a fact that was incongruous with the city's thriving textile industry and India's newfound independence.

Vikram's return from his second stint at Cambridge was pivotal in transforming this plan into reality. Kasturbhai, recognising Vikram's unique position as both a trained scientist and a member of a leading mill-owning family, tasked him with studying industrial research structures in the UK and Europe for implementation in India. Vikram's involvement with ATIRA exemplified his commitment to applied science, a theme he often highlighted in his speeches. He believed that the greatest advancements in science and technology came from the interplay between basic and practical problems.

In 1966, during a lecture at Rockefeller University in New York, Vikram reiterated his belief in the practical application of intellectual endeavours, expressing concern over the isolation of research scientists and academics. He emphasised the importance of those capable of posing basic questions also engaging in applied work.

However, Vikram's role in ATIRA also highlighted a familial pattern: while the women in the Sarabhai family often challenged feudalism and patriarchy, the men, despite their progressive views, did not actively address class inequality. Mridula, Vikram's cousin, was acutely aware of the labour issues, evident in her diary entries, about the growing discontent among workers. Vikram, however, aligned himself more closely with the mill owners.

ATIRA was formally established in December 1947, initially operating from the AMA building. A large 75-acre plot at Gujarat University was allocated for the new institute. Lockwood Green of New York was contracted for the project report and laboratory plans, and Achyut Kanvinde, principal architect for CSIR, along with his associate Shankar Rai, began the planning process. In the interim, a small team comprising a mathematical statistician, a social psychologist, a high-polymer chemist, and a physical chemist started their work in temporary premises at MG Science College. While Vikram was the driving force behind ATIRA, another project was simultaneously evolving, capturing a significant portion of his attention and time.

More About ATIRA at the Present Time.

The ATIRA, with its voluntary membership, has become a pivotal institution in India's textile sector. Boasting 146 member units both in India and abroad, ATIRA's network is quite extensive. This ensemble includes 93 units specialising in ginning, spinning, weaving, process houses, and composite textile units. Additionally, 53 members are manufacturers of fibres, dyes, chemicals, instruments, equipment, and machinery, highlighting the broad spectrum of the textile industry that ATIRA encompasses.

ATIRA's financial backbone is supported by four primary sources. These include annual subscriptions from member units, income generated from the services it offers, sponsored research from the industry, and grant aid from the government of India. Notably, the Ministry of Textiles and the Ministry of Information Technology, along with other agencies like the Gujarat state government, play a significant role in sponsoring ATIRA's research initiatives.

Governance at ATIRA is overseen by a seventeen-member council. This council is a blend of industry and government representation, consisting of five elected members from the industry (including the chairman), three nominated members from various departments of the government of India, and three designated scientists. The council also includes a representative from the associate members, the president of the Ahmedabad Textile Mills Association, and the four directors of Cotton Textile Research Associations as ex-officio members, which includes the director of ATIRA.

Currently, ATIRA has 91 units as members across India, including 10 original or privileged members and 81 associate members. The location of ATIRA is strategic, situated near several prominent research and educational institutions like the Indian Institute of Management Ahmedabad, the Physical Research Laboratory, and Gujarat University. Its campus spans 272,000 square metres, dotted with over 1,000 trees, making it a favoured spot for morning walks and jogging among locals.

The foundation of ATIRA's complex, a significant landmark, was laid by Vallabhbhai Patel on 1 November 1950 and was inaugurated by then Prime Minister Jawaharlal Nehru on 10 April 1954. The architect responsible for the design of the ATIRA building was Achyut Kanvinde, whose work was influenced by

Walter Gropius, a renowned architect known for his modernist approach. This architectural lineage adds a historical and cultural significance to the ATIRA complex, making it not just a centre for textile research but also a monument of modern architectural heritage.

*****

In the early decades of the twentieth century, distinguished scientists such as Raman, Saha and Jagadish Chandra Bose marked a pivotal era in the scientific landscape. However, the prevailing condition of scientific facilities in India during this period, particularly in the university settings, was not reflective of their prominence. Despite the efforts of independent benefactors like DrMahendra Lal Sircar, who established the Indian Association for the Cultivation of Science in Calcutta—a hub where Raman conducted his groundbreaking research—the overall prioritisation of scientific studies in universities was lacking.

Notably, Calcutta University did not boast a science department until 1914, and financial constraints compelled the construction of the college building with economical materials. A telling example of the inadequate state of affairs was Meghnad Saha's experience when he assumed the role of head of physics at Allahabad University in the 1920s. The absence of an essential research apparatus and an electricity-deprived workshop illustrated the uphill battle in fostering scientific exploration. Saha's attempt to procure additional books for the library was met with the directive to exhaust the existing collection first.

By 1945, the landscape began to transform with the establishment of Bhabha's Tata Institute for Fundamental Research (TIFR), followed by the inception of national laboratories. Yet, in a country as vast as India, opportunities for advanced research remained scarce. Against this backdrop, Vikram's decision to establish his own laboratory, the Physical Research Laboratory (PRL), is noteworthy. According to his wife, Mrinalini, Vikram conceived the idea for PRL during his stint as a student in England between 1937 and 1940, formulating the institute's entire research programme during a train journey.

However, the timeline presented by Mrinalini seems improbable, considering Raman's influence in steering Vikram toward his field of research and the latter's groundbreaking discovery of time variations in Kashmir. These findings laid the foundation for subsequent investigations at PRL. It is more plausible that Vikram's conceptualisation of PRL occurred during his second phase at Cambridge, following interactions with luminaries such as Raman, Bhabha and Ramanathan, coupled with his in-depth exploration of cosmic rays. This scenario aligns with the swift implementation of his plans upon his return in 1947.

Vikram's initial aspirations were characterised by a sense of modesty, reflecting a recurring pattern in his approach. Despite the grandeur of his vision, his practical demeanour mirrored the cautious pragmatism ingrained in Ahmedabadi business culture. Adhering to his belief in incremental growth, he opted to commence on a small scale. In the case of the Physical Research Laboratory (PRL), this translated into the relocation of the workshop from 'The Retreat', a place where he had spent his childhood operating lathes and drills, to the service quarters behind the main building of MG Science College.

The Ahmedabad Education Society (AES), under the stewardship of Kasturbhai Lalbhai, generously contributed land for a new building, supplemented by support from the Sarabhais' Karmakshetra Educational Foundation. In November 1947, PRL began its operations, with rudimentary facilities that included a makeshift table crafted from asbestos sheets and a few racks serving as the 'library'. Vikram's room occupied a passage, embodying the essence of a humble beginning. Notably, KR Ramanathan, the seasoned deputy director general of the Poona

Observatory, responded to Vikram's invitation post-retirement, assuming the pivotal roles of director and professor of atmospheric physics in March 1948.

The word about the nascent laboratory quickly spread. At that time, existing science institutes were predominantly preoccupied with classical physics domains like heat and thermodynamics. Institutes led by luminaries like Raman in Bangalore and others in Benares were centred on spectroscopy. For ambitious young students eager to delve into the cutting-edge realms of nuclear and cosmic ray physics, viable opportunities were scarce. Nevertheless, as word spread, students began to trickle in, each encountering Vikram's immediate and profound influence.

Take the case of Praful Bhavsar, an atypical research student, and the son of a businessman facing financial challenges. Driven by his fervour for nuclear physics, Bhavsar embarked on a fruitless search from Bombay to Poona until Dr LA Ramdas, deputy director general of the India Meteorological Department, directed him to PRL andVikram. Arriving in August 1948, Bhavsar found Vikram in a small room, clad in 'white khaddar trousers and a bright green shirt', engaged in repairing a Geiger counter at the glass-blower's desk. Vikram's warm greeting and unassuming demeanour left a lasting impression on Bhavsar, who was immediately drawn to this 'very simple, unassuming person' fitting the mental image of a young experimental physicist in his mind.

In January, during the Indian Science Congress in Allahabad, a pivotal moment unfolded for RG Rastogi, a lecturer at Sagar University. He was encouraged by Sydney Chapman, a distinguished geophysics expert who had recently delivered a series of enlightening lectures on geomagnetism at the Physical Research Laboratory (PRL). Chapman urged Rastogi to keep an eye out for a young man, seemingly pursued by a group of eager students, who had initiated an intriguing new laboratory venture in Ahmedabad. Rastogi took Chapman's advice to heart and, almost inevitably, found himself captivated by the prospects of this exciting opportunity. It wasn't long before he made the life-altering decision to resign from his current job and join PRL.

Meanwhile, EV Chitnis, a well-paid engineer at All India Radio, was making a significant career shift. Despite his comfortable income, he decided to leave his position and align his destiny with Vikram, accepting a modest monthly scholarship of Rs 100 in 1951. UR Rao, equipped with an MSc from Benares, followed suit in 1953. Over the intervening years, individuals like RP Kane, Satya Prakash, and UD Desai joined the ranks, each bringing their unique talents and perspectives to PRL. BHV Raman Murthy and JV Dave also heeded the call to collaborate with Dr Ramanathan.

However, PRL faced limitations when it came to providing scholarships, and it was not uncommon for students, often at Vikram's suggestion, to seek employment as demonstrators at local colleges. After a day's work, they would make their way to PRL, where they balanced their scientific pursuits with cooking their meals on hotplates amidst the backdrop of their electronic devices.

In February 1952, a momentous event occurred as the foundation stone for a new laboratory building was laid. This momentous occasion was graced by luminaries such as CV Raman, SSBhatnagar from CSIR, Homi Bhabha, and Kasturbhai Lalbhai. The main building was officially inaugurated in April 1954, with none other than Jawaharlal Nehru, a close family friend of Vikram, presiding over the ceremony. However, even before these grand ceremonies took place, the work was already in full swing.

The study of cosmic rays played a central role in the scientific endeavours at PRL. These high-energy particles spend more than 2.5 million years in interstellar space, where continuous interactions with magnetic fields cause them to lose their original directionality. Consequently, when they enter our solar system, they exhibit isotropic behaviour, displaying uniform density in all directions. Nevertheless, as they encounter interplanetary magnetic fields within our solar system, they undergo transformations that disrupt their isotropic nature. Vikram and his fellow scientists working in this field recognised that precise measurements of the variations in cosmic ray intensity over time and space could yield valuable insights into the electromagnetic conditions of interplanetary space.

In the 1940s, the path to understanding these phenomena was far from clear. Initially, Vikram, like many others, entertained the idea that fluctuations in cosmic ray intensity might be attributed to a continuous emission of cosmic ray particles by the sun. However, by the mid-1950s, he became increasingly convinced of the existence of electromagnetic fields in interplanetary space.

At the outset, their efforts were concentrated on comprehending the nature of these variations. During his second phase at the Indian Institute of Science (IISc), Vikram meticulously designed an intricate apparatus that featured various configurations of Geiger counters. This apparatus was intended to record cosmic ray intensities at hourly intervals, and it was no easy task given that the fluctuations were minute, often not exceeding 1 percent. Moreover, to obtain accurate data, the influence of meteorological conditions had to be meticulously accounted for. Just before he departed for Cambridge, Vikram had relocated this experiment to the Poona Observatory to gain a deeper understanding of the meteorological data. At PRL, the initial steps were focused on building upon these preliminary investigations, setting the stage for groundbreaking discoveries in the field of cosmic ray research.

Following Vikram's meticulous instructions, his dedicated students embarked on a challenging endeavour: the creation of a series of Geiger counter telescopes. These ingenious devices were constructed using one-and-a-half-foot-long cylinders and lead plates, and a recording station was meticulously set up to monitor the cosmic ray variations. Simultaneously, KR Ramanathan, armed with his knowledge of meteorological factors, formulated a comprehensive method for measuring atmospheric variables in both the surface and upper atmosphere.

The magnitude of this undertaking demanded an exceptional degree of patience and unwavering concentration. It was akin to the analogy Vikram often favoured—Listening for music in a stormy sky. At PRL, the path was strewn with obstacles of diverse natures. One of Vikram's students, RP Kane, vividly describes the challenges they faced:

"Day in and day out, we diligently recorded data, initially through manual means, later transitioning to photographic and automated methods. The cosmic ray rates exhibited variations throughout the day, sometimes fluctuating by as much as 10-15 percent. Yet, these deviations could all be attributed to loose wiring causing unreliable connections, frequently disrupted by the multitude of pigeons that had taken up residence in the MG Science Institute. These feathered inhabitants would often perch on the telescope, causing noticeable tremors. Furthermore, the stability of our main power supply left much to be desired. Voltage fluctuations were rampant, and our power sources struggled to cope. Consequently, the cosmic ray rates fluctuated on all days, except for Sundays when power demand was lower, and mains stability improved."

When the students raised concerns about these hindrances, Vikram simply shrugged his shoulders, sporting a knowing smile, and encouraged them to press on. The work continued relentlessly. Gradually, refinements were made to the instruments. The Geiger counter telescopes were elongated to three feet, and solutions were devised to counter both the avian interference and the erratic electrical supply. In 1949, Vikram extended his operations to establish another recording station at a higher altitude in the picturesque hill station of Kodaikanal. Finally, after months of painstaking observations and meticulous data collection, a pattern emerged—a wavy, semi-diurnal structure of variations.

With a sense of pride, Vikram presented these findings to his colleague Homi Bhabha during one of his visits. However, Bhabha, known for his exacting standards, was not easily impressed. He questioned the margin of error and expressed uncertainty about the absence of a horizontal line through the data points. Vikram, ever undaunted, responded calmly, "Yes, Homi, the errors are indeed quite substantial. We will address this issue."

True to his word, Vikram initiated significant enhancements. Super neutron monitors and large-area, scintillation telescopes were installed at the recording stations to enhance precision. In 1954, a sea-level station was added in Trivandrum, further expanding the scope of their research.

Despite the perceived brusqueness of Homi Bhabha, it is evident that he harboured a sympathetic understanding of Vikram's relentless pursuit of scientific excellence. As early as 1945, Bhabha had established the Tata Institute of Fundamental Research (TIFR), destined to be the cradle of India's atomic energy programme. By 1946, he chaired the Atomic Energy Research Committee. In 1948, shortly after India's independence, Jawaharlal Nehru introduced the Atomic Energy Act before the Constituent Assembly. On 10 August 1948, a mere year after independence, the Atomic Energy Commission (AEC) was established, with a three-member committee. In 1954, Bhabha was appointed as the secretary of the newly formed Department of Atomic Energy (DAE). In his role as DAE secretary, Bhabha offered unwavering support to Vikram and his groundbreaking cosmic ray research.

A Little Insight on PRL

The Physical Research Laboratory (PRL) is a prominent National Research Institute located in Ahmedabad, India, dedicated to space and allied sciences. Established on 11 November 1947, by the visionary Dr Vikram Sarabhai, PRL had humble beginnings, with its early research focus centred on cosmic rays. Over the years, it has evolved into a multifaceted institution with ongoing research programmes in various domains.

PRL's research endeavours encompass a wide range of scientific disciplines, including astronomy and astrophysics, atmospheric sciences and aeronomy, planetary and geosciences, Earth sciences, solar system studies, and theoretical physics. It also oversees and manages the Udaipur Solar Observatory and Mount Abu InfraRed Observatory, both contributing significantly to our understanding of the cosmos.

One of PRL's notable achievements occurred in June 2018 when its scientists made a groundbreaking discovery by identifying the exoplanet EPIC 211945201b, also known as K2-236b, located an astonishing 600 light years away from Earth. This discovery marked a significant milestone in the field of astronomy and showcased PRL's dedication to advancing our knowledge of the universe.

The architectural magnificence of PRL's building, designed by Achyut Kanvinde in 1962, is complemented by a well-structured organisational hierarchy. At the apex of this hierarchy is the PRL Council of Management, overseeing the institute's operations. The director of PRL operates under its guidance, collaborating with various scientific divisions, the dean, and the registrar to ensure the institution's consistent progress.

PRL is divided into several scientific divisions, each dedicated to specific research areas. These divisions include Astronomy & Astrophysics, Solar Physics, Planetary Sciences, Space

& Atmospheric Sciences, Geosciences, Theoretical Physics, and Atomic, Molecular & Optical Physics. These divisions engage in interdisciplinary research, exploring topics such as astrochemistry, quantum mechanics' foundations, luminescence dating, and much more. The institute boasts a wide array of experimental facilities, from diode-pumped solid-state lasers to spectroscopy equipment, supporting its extensive research endeavours.

The Planetary Sciences division at PRL delves into the characterisation of processes that occurred in the early solar system, employing stable and radioactive isotopes. Their research aims to unravel the origin and evolution of the solar system, with a specific focus on the inner planets. Additionally, they explore the physical and chemical processes in planetary atmospheres through simulations, observations and modelling. The Planetary Science and Exploration Programme (PLANEX) is a noteworthy initiative under this division.

The Theoretical Physics Division at PRL conducts research on atomic physics, condensed matter physics, gravitation, astroparticle physics, and various other theoretical and phenomenological aspects of physics. Their programmes include studies on neutrino physics, particle physics beyond the standard model, and quantum chaos in nuclear energy levels, among others.

The Space and Atmospheric Sciences Division at PRL is dedicated to studying various processes in Earth's atmosphere using a combination of in-situ rocket and balloon-borne experiments, laboratory research, simulations, and modelling. Their research domains span atmospheric chemistry, aerosols, radiation, climate and plasma interactions in near-Earth space. They employ an impressive array of experimental equipment, including lidar and greenhouse gas analysers.

The Geosciences Division at PRL specialises in geochronology, geochemistry, glaciology, oceanography and paleoclimatology. They explore Earth's origin and evolution, with a particular emphasis on isotope geology. This division conducts research programmes in areas such as aerosol chemistry, hydrology and oceanography, supported by advanced equipment like accelerator mass spectrometers and ion chromatographs.

In essence, the Physical Research Laboratory stands as a beacon of scientific excellence, continually pushing the boundaries of knowledge in the realms of space and allied sciences. With its pioneering research, state-of-the-art facilities, and dedicated team of scientists, PRL continues to make remarkable contributions to our understanding of the universe and our planet.

❑

Some Other Chapters of His Life

While Vikram Sarabhai was deeply engaged in establishing the first among his numerous educational and research institutions, his wife Mrinalini, a talented dancer, rejuvenated her dancing career. Following their return from England, encouraged by Vikram, she gathered a group of dancers and musicians from Bangalore, forming her own dance company. In the traditionally conservative society of Ahmedabad, the idea of a Sarabhai daughter-in-law performing dance publicly was met with some surprise, yet this did not impede her flourishing career. In 1949, a prominent local impresario, impressed by her performance, recommended her to the organisers of a prestigious festival in Paris. This resulted in an invitation for a performance. Vikram, supportive as ever, encouraged her to accept the invitation and travelled with her to Paris, along with their young son Kartikeya and a nanny. What was initially planned as a single performance evolved into a full-fledged tour. The European press was captivated, endearingly referring to Mrinalini as 'Les Bomb Atomique des Hindous' and Vikram as 'the Indian Joliot-Curie', a nod to the son-in-law of the famed Marie Curie, known for his work in artificial radioactivity.

Back in Ahmedabad, the Sarabhais' social life was vibrant and illustrious. They resided at 'The Retreat', mingling with the city's elite, including Vikram's lifelong friend Chinubhai Lalbhai and his artistic wife Prabha, Vikram's sister Leena, and prominent local industrialists like Navneet Shodhan, Harshvardhan Mangaldas, and Baronet Udayan. Their social calendar was filled with elaborate dinner parties, treasure hunts, and themed fancy dress events. Vikram was once photographed at one of these events, donning a kabuki mask and gloves. The Gymkhana Club was a frequent haunt for them, where they often indulged in ballroom dancing, excelling in dances like the foxtrot and the waltz, alongside the remaining British families in the city. Traditional festivities like Makar Sankranti were celebrated with kite flying on the terraces of local mansions in the pols.

During this period, the Sarabhai family's fortunes were growing exponentially. The year 1947 had been particularly prosperous for their Calico Mills enterprise, with Ambalal Sarabhai's success showing no signs of waning. Since 1940, Vikram's elder brother Gautam, a Cambridge alumnus with a background in philosophy and mathematics, had joined the family business, bringing fresh, innovative ideas. Gautam had even engaged a consultant from London's renowned Tavistock Institute to introduce advanced management techniques and had implemented Buckminster Fuller's geodesic dome design at the Calico Mills. Bharti Sarabhai, following her return from England, also began to show an active interest in the family's business ventures.

Vikram Sarabhai, while charting his distinct professional course, seemed to maintain a connection with his family's business interests. In Bangalore, he encountered MS Sastry, a chemistry lecturer at Central College, during events at the Indian Institute of Science (IISc). Sastry recounts an unexpected suggestion from Vikram to apply for a position with the Sarabhai enterprises in Ahmedabad, which advice he followed, leading to a successful job acquisition.

This incident indicates that even during his student years, Vikram was vigilant in scouting talent beneficial for his family's enterprises, hinting that his involvement in the family business might not have been as unlikely as it appeared. In 1950, this possibility materialised when Vikram took over as chairman of Sarabhai Chemicals, a pharmaceutical company based in Baroda. The transition of leadership from Ambalal to Vikram was smooth, and his approach to intertwining the business with his technological and nationalistic aspirations suggests prior deliberation both within the family and in Vikram's mind.

Vikram's role required weekly travel to Baroda to oversee the Sarabhai Chemicals plant, a journey he made by train due to the lack of a road connection between Ahmedabad and Baroda. He often invited a student from the Physical Research Laboratory (PRL) to accompany him, utilising the travel time for academic discussions. These trips allowed the students to understand their mentor better, as Vikram would candidly share his concerns for India and his ambition to transform societal patterns. They also observed his fondness for local snacks, despite his struggles with resisting them.

In addition to his professional endeavours, Vikram also made time for personal connections. He regularly visited Mrinalini's cousin, Vinodini, who had relocated to Baroda after her marriage. His consistent visits, every Thursday at four, were likely at Mrinalini's behest. Initially, Vinodini felt overwhelmed hosting Vikram and his companions in her modest apartment. However, Vikram's unpretentious and sociable nature quickly put her at ease, making these visits a comfortable and familiar routine.

Up to this point in his life, Vikram Sarabhai had been methodically laying the groundwork for his future endeavours.

He was a family man, married with two children, and had founded the Physical Research Laboratory (PRL), which would become central to his numerous achievements. Despite his future renown in various fields, Sarabhai often acknowledged that it was in scientific research that he found his true passion and fulfilment. Alongside his work at PRL, he also served as a visiting professor at MIT in Boston during the summers.

The laboratory at MIT, headed by Bruno Rossi, was at the forefront of X-ray astronomy and space plasma physics. It attracted physicists involved in defence work during World War II and scientists from around the globe, including France, Italy, China, Japan and Australia. Sarabhai and his PRL team were regular visitors, fostering a strong reciprocal relationship between the two institutions. Nora Rossi, Bruno Rossi's wife, fondly remembered the springs in Boston when Sarabhai would arrive, enlivening their days and evenings with his enthusiasm, vivacity and charm.

Sarabhai's dedication to pure science did not diminish his commitment to his other responsibilities. In fact, his scientific rigour seemed to enhance his ability to initiate and develop projects efficiently. He believed that the early stages of any institution were critical and that the culture set by the initial members significantly influenced its norms, procedures and practices.

However, establishing a strong foundation was not without its challenges. This was evident in his experiences with the ATIRA. Appointed as the honorary director in 1949, Sarabhai faced the task of assembling a team. He recruited nearly 70 people, most of whom, like him, were young and inexperienced in textile manufacturing. His decision to prioritise fresh, scientific minds over trained technologists was deliberate, as it was unlikely to find individuals with the exact qualifications needed at the time. The skills necessary for an organisation like ATIRA were not readily available, requiring a degree of adaptability. Thus, individuals with diverse backgrounds, like someone with a degree in statistics or a physicist, found themselves developing expertise in areas like spinning technology and textile manufacturing, respectively.

MM Gharia, who joined the ATIRA in the 1950s and eventually became its director, reflects on Vikram Sarabhai's approach: "Vikrambhai caught them young and groomed them." This statement underscores Sarabhai's strategy of nurturing young talent to foster innovation and progress within ATIRA.

By February 1952, ATIRA had established a pilot mill, equipped with machinery and facilities to simulate the actual operations of a textile mill. The early studies conducted there led to significant findings, suggesting solutions to problems long considered endemic in the industry. For instance, one study revealed that the low productivity in spinning was largely due to poor maintenance of machinery and the absence of process controls. Another study proposed methods to reduce cotton wastage. Innovatively, tamarind kernel powder, an agricultural by-product, was tested as a substitute for starch in the process. There were also suggestions for improving ginning and weaving techniques, reducing humidification costs, and conserving energy. These innovations were projected to save an estimated Rs 20 crore over the next two decades, a substantial part of which would be in foreign exchange.

The pragmatic mill owners of Ahmedabad, initially persuaded by Kasturbhai to contribute Rs 50 lakh, had every reason to be satisfied with these developments. However, their reaction was surprisingly negative.

At first glance, this negative response from the mill owners seemed paradoxical. ATIRA, the organisation they had funded, was offering them the prospect of better returns and increased efficiency. The root of their dissatisfaction lay in their traditional business practices. Ahmedabad's business community traditionally relied on instinct and empirical methods. Sarabhai's advocacy for adopting a scientific approach—as he emphasised at the association's first technological conference—was to base operations on rational understanding and systematic inquiry, rather than on an empirical, trial-and-error basis. This shift towards a methodical and questioning approach was a significant departure from their customary practices.

This transition to a scientific methodology was unsettling for those accustomed to empirical operations. ATIRA's move towards understanding and standardising practices was seen as a challenge to traditional methods, which did not sit well with the established business leaders, or Sheths. As ATIRA's research team began to assert their ideas, perhaps too assertively, sections of the industry started to protest. This resentment became evident during board meetings, where Vikram's methods were openly criticised. Facing opposition from community elders was likely an unpleasant experience for Sarabhai, but his busy schedule and myriad commitments may have prevented him from dwelling too heavily on these challenges.

Vikram Sarabhai's routine was a testament to his dedication and meticulous work ethic. He started his days early, often reaching the PRL by seven in the morning, his punctuality so consistent that local residents claimed they could set their clocks by his arrival. His small, self-driven Standard car became a familiar sight on his morning route. On Mondays, late in the morning, he dedicated his time to meetings with the senior staff at the ATIRA. Other days were filled with overseeing ongoing construction activities at both PRL and ATIRA, followed by visits to the Calico building around noon. There, in his office adorned with coir matting, he would attend to matters related to Sarabhai Chemicals and meet with visitors who were well aware of his busy schedule and often prepared for long waits. In the evenings, Vikram enjoyed a brief respite, socialising or listening to music on hi-fi equipment he had assembled from parts acquired abroad. However, his commitment to PRL often saw him returning to work shortly after.

During this period, Vikram's wife, Mrinalini Sarabhai, known as Darpana, was achieving international acclaim in her dance career. In 1950, the government of India sponsored her tour to Egypt, followed by a tour to South America in 1951. Vikram joined her in Mexico City along with their four-year-old son Kartikeya, staying in a Spanish hacienda and exploring the locale. By 1954, Darpana had embarked on an extensive tour of thirty-eight cities in Europe. During her absence, Vikram would sometimes visit his friend Chinubhai's house for lunch, where he would relax and engage in conversations. Chinubhai's wife Prabha recalled these visits, noting Vikram's apparent loneliness without his wife.

Back at ATIRA, Vikram faced continued challenges. Despite the ongoing impasse and resistance from the mill owners and technicians, he remained resolute. His efforts were bolstered by the supportive attitude of Kasturbhai Lalbhai. The technicians, sceptical of ATIRA's staff whom they suspected of being spies for management, refused to cooperate, posing further obstacles to Vikram's initiatives.

Anticipating these challenges, Vikram had wisely included an industrial psychology division at ATIRA. This division played a crucial role in facilitating the integration of new practices by addressing the human aspects of implementing change. PC Mehta, a former director of ATIRA, credited this division with significantly aiding the physical scientists in understanding the complexities of introducing changes in a traditional industry.

A notable member of the industrial psychology division was Kamla Chowdhry. She was a slim, dusky Punjabi Khatri woman from a respected family in Lahore, her features reflecting a blend of attractiveness and resilience. In a time when it was uncommon for Indian women to relocate alone for work, Kamla's background was extraordinary. She had been married to an Indian Civil Service (ICS) officer who was tragically killed three months into their marriage. Finding herself a widow at the age of twenty, Kamla made the unconventional decision to further her education. Switching her field of study from mathematics to psychology, she earned her Master's and later pursued a PhD in Michigan, USA. Her decision to join ATIRA in Ahmedabad was a bold and pioneering step for a woman in her situation during that era.

Kasturbhai Lalbhai, a family friend and prominent figure, was instrumental in introducing Kamla Chowdhry to ATIRA. He informed her about an opening in the psychology department, which she applied for despite her relatives' scepticism about her prospects in Ahmedabad. Kamla was selected to lead the department and quickly found herself immersed in the world of textile workers, addressing their concerns and challenges. Her role was crucial in bridging the gap between the workers and ATIRA's scientists, who were eager for information to advance their studies. Vikram Sarabhai ensured her safety and comfort, often sending his driver and a flask of coffee, reflecting his natural tendency towards solicitousness, especially since Kamla was a close friend of his wife, Mrinalini.

Kamla and Mrinalini had been fellow students at Santiniketan and maintained contact over the years. Vikram's connection with Kamla dated back to an encounter at Lahore station during a trip north, possibly in 1943, when Mrinalini had asked Kamla to meet them with milk and fruit. This early interaction laid the foundation for their subsequent professional relationship at ATIRA.

Under Vikram's patient guidance, the initial resistance from the technicians and other stakeholders at ATIRA began to diminish. His approach eventually transformed him from a scapegoat to a unifying force, bridging the divide between technicians, scientists, mill owners and the government. In recognition of his sensitivity and understanding of their concerns, the Textile Technicians' Association invited him to become their president in 1955, marking the first time a mill owner had been honoured in this way.

Vikram's leadership at ATIRA fostered a deep sense of loyalty and belonging among his team, a pattern that was consistent across all his enterprises. Most employees who began their careers at ATIRA remained until retirement, inspired by a strong sense of pride in the organisation. This sentiment was likely a reflection of Vikram's own attitude. Gharia recalls how Vikram was actively involved in maintaining the new ATIRA building, which boasted modern facilities like laboratories, offices and a centrally air-conditioned cafeteria—a novelty at the time. Vikram's hands-on approach even extended to ensuring the building's upkeep, demonstrating his commitment to every aspect of the organisation.

Vikram's management style was characterised by his pursuit of 'mutuality' in all his endeavours. He believed in treating people as ends in themselves, not merely as means to an end. This philosophy was central to his interactions with staff and colleagues. Kamla, reflecting on Vikram's managerial qualities, highlighted his ability to imbue a sense of purpose and challenge in his team. He encouraged young people to take risks and protected them from potential harm, fostering a culture of strong teamwork and integrity. This approach not only built a loyal and dedicated workforce but also instilled a sense of shared mission and ethical conduct in those who worked with him.

The narrative of Vikram Sarabhai's life at this juncture presents a complex interplay of professional dedication, personal relationships, and emotional dynamics. His emphasis on recruiting young talent and fostering a conducive working culture was rooted in a belief system he called the 'three raised to the power of eighteen' theory. This theory posited that a small core group of motivated individuals could exponentially expand their influence, ultimately creating a significant social impact, akin to an avalanche. This approach was evident in his leadership at institutions like ATIRA and PRL.

Kamla Chowdhry, having joined ATIRA and frequently visited Vikram's home, became increasingly close to him, especially during Mrinalini Sarabhai's frequent absences. This growing intimacy between Kamla and Vikram raised questions about the dynamics of his marriage with Mrinalini. Mrinalini, a vibrant and independent individual, had her own complex emotional landscape, shaped by early personal losses and a sense of loneliness. This, coupled with Vikram's seemingly over-attentive involvement in her career, created an intricate marital relationship.

The situation with Kamla brought an added layer of complexity. Known for her unpredictable nature and battling her own past traumas, Kamla was a strong yet emotionally intricate personality. Vikram, who appeared to be drawn to intelligent women with complex emotional backgrounds, found in Kamla a person requiring support and understanding, mirroring his protective and nurturing role in professional contexts.

The proposition by Vikram to Kamla, asking her to accompany him to Kashmir, marked a significant turn in their relationship. Kamla, despite her initial hesitation and after consulting with the wife of a visiting MIT professor, decided to join him, indicating the depth of their connection and her inability to resist the pull of this relationship.

This phase of Vikram's life, marked by his professional achievements and personal entanglements, reflects the multifaceted nature of human relationships and the complexities inherent in balancing personal desires, professional obligations, and emotional needs. It underscores how personal dynamics can be as intricate and challenging as professional endeavours, especially for individuals in positions of influence and responsibility like Vikram Sarabhai.

❑

Developing Ahmedabad

On the memorable evening of 1 May 1960, the vibrant city of Ahmedabad was cloaked in an atmosphere of jubilation. Servants were seen distributing sweets to delighted children, a gesture that symbolised the city's celebration of the historic formation of Gujarat as an independent state. This significant event was commemorated that morning with a vivid and festive ceremony held at Gandhi's former prayer ground in Ahmedabad, marking a pivotal moment in the region's history. This ceremony was the formal acknowledgement of Gujarat's separation from the larger Bombay Presidency, to which it had belonged until that day. Meanwhile, across the newly formed boundary, the Marathi-speaking populace in the residual areas of the erstwhile Presidency was equally immersed in festivities, joyously marking the birth of their state, Maharashtra.

The genesis of federal India had been unfolding throughout the 1950s, a decade marked by the rise of regional aspirations post-independence. Among these aspirations, the linguistic element was particularly influential. The fragmentation of the Bombay Presidency was the climax of a passionate and sometimes violent five-year campaign that had intensified regional, parochial and linguistic fervour in both Gujarat and Maharashtra. In Ahmedabad, now the capital of the newly established Gujarat, the most enthusiastic applause was reserved for Ravi Shanker Maharaj. This esteemed Sarvodaya leader was celebrated for his extensive travels to every village in the state during the agitation, an effort that was widely acknowledged and revered.

Conversely, the escalating regional agitation seemed to have a negligible impact on the elite of Ahmedabad. At a time when Gujarat's political leaders and activists were vigorously advocating for a reinvigoration of ethnic identity, the affluent Ahmedabadi Sheths (business leaders) appeared to be embracing broader, more global influences. By this era, the younger generation of mill owners, also known as 'managing agents', were increasingly seeking education abroad, predominantly in England and the United States. Their lifestyles began to reflect a fusion of Eastern and Western influences. Furthermore, many of the professional technicians employed in their mills were recruited from regions where expertise in engineering and mechanics was more readily available. At conferences organised by institutions like ATIRA, where Vikram had stepped down as director in 1956 but remained actively involved, there was a strong emphasis on inviting external experts to share their knowledge. This initiative underscored a growing openness among the Sheths, although the depth of this openness remained a subject of contemplation.

The visits of two illustrious figures to Ahmedabad in the late 1950s and early 1960s provide insightful glimpses into the social and cultural dynamics of the city during this transformative period. Prakash Tandon, who would later ascend to the prestigious position of heading Unilever's Indian operations, was a senior executive at the company during his visit. He was among the select hundred guests from outside the city invited to the annual conference of ATIRA in 1957. His experiences at this conference are vividly detailed in his autobiography.

Tandon observed that the conference followed the usual format of such gatherings in India, yet it was distinctive in its comprehensive approach. It included keynote speeches, votes of thanks, talks, group discussions, seminars, presentations by seminar leaders, open discussions, a plenary session, and a summarisation. Despite the variety of activities, Tandon noted a harmonious rhythm in the proceedings, with a unanimous accord in the views expressed. Speeches were delivered with heartfelt sincerity, emphasising the importance of understanding and valuing the roles of workers and managers, and advocating for their consultation, delegation and promotion. However, Tandon expressed scepticism about the practical application of these ideals in India's highly structured and hierarchical society, suggesting that such democratic management principles might be more theoretical than practical.

In the evenings, Tandon and other guests were hosted at the homes of Ahmedabad's elders. These gatherings, held in exquisite homes, offered an array of spicy and sweet non-alcoholic drinks, soups served in teacups, and a mix of Indian and Continental cuisine presented on silver and Royal Doulton china. The evenings concluded promptly at nine, leaving Tandon pondering the nature of this impeccable yet somewhat impersonal hospitality, which he perceived as a form of self-imposed social obligation.

A few years later, the renowned psychoanalyst Erik Erikson visited Ahmedabad. His first trip was in 1962 to attend an ATIRA conference, and he returned in 1963 to conduct research for a book on Gandhi's early political activities, focusing mainly on the textile strike of 1918. During both his visits, Erikson was a guest of the Sarabhai family. On one occasion, when his wife Joan fell ill with dysentery, their crisis was met with an outpouring of support. A dedicated group, including several members of the host family, the chief of internal medicine from the medical school, the head doctor of the mills, and the chief secretary of the state of Gujarat, swiftly gathered at their residence at 'The Retreat' to provide assistance. This incident underscores the hospitality and community spirit prevalent among Ahmedabad's elite during this era.

Erik Erikson's account of his experience in Ahmedabad, particularly during his wife's illness, is tinged with a mix of bemusement and appreciation. He recounts with a hint of amused bewilderment how the discussion about his wife's condition unfolded in Gujarati, with an air of urgency and gravity. After briefly seeking Erikson's agreement, Sarla, their host, took swift action. She left with three servants to prepare a hospital room, ensuring it was adorned with flowers and equipped with fresh bed sheets. Following these preparations, Erikson describes Sarla returning in her limousine to transport his wife, Joan, to the hospital.

Both Tandon's and Erikson's narratives offer unique insights into the world of the Ahmedabadi elite, a realm that was both exclusive and nurtured Vikram until that point in his life. These insights are particularly valuable due to their rare accessibility and the objective perspective of the observers. Prakash Tandon, with his robust Punjabi-corporate background, and Erik Erikson, armed with his acute analytical skills, both perceived a certain stiffness or rigidity in the atmosphere among the Ahmedabadi elite. This community was noted for its excessive hospitality, as Tandon observed, offering generous hospitality without expecting anything in return. Erikson, on his part, experienced an extreme level of care and attention.

However, this was only part of the broader narrative. Vikram's experiences at ATIRA had already hinted that the Ahmedabadi entrepreneurs, while quick to extend a friendly gesture, were inherently cautious and required convincing to embrace change. The experiences of both Tandon and Erikson further illuminate another aspect: an underlying patronising attitude among the wealthy mill owners. This attitude welcomed outsiders but simultaneously instilled a sense of discomfort in them.

In the case of the Sarabhai family, this feeling was perhaps accentuated by their high-minded goals. Both Ambalal and Sarla Sarabhai were extraordinary individuals who had carved out a unique niche in their pursuit of excellence. Erikson notes the striking simplicity yet elegance of their attire and the respect they commanded at public events. However, he also sensed their somewhat isolated position from their peers, perceiving them as 'stubborn and somewhat self-righteous', albeit tempered by their personal experiences with the rigid orthodoxies of their caste and social milieu.

Vikram, a member of this family, appears to have inherited some of these traits. For instance, at the young age of 23, following his expedition to Kashmir, he confidently proposed to scientists and government departments the idea of establishing a permanent high-altitude laboratory in the Himalayas, displaying a certain boldness and conviction characteristic of his family lineage.

Vikram's personality was a complex tapestry of traits, notably marked by his tremendous self-confidence and precocious maturity. His early fascination with philosophy and a persistent drive to transform his ideas into tangible institutions further defined his character. Additionally, his penchant for meticulously documenting his non-scientific experiments and theorising them seemed to stem from his scientific background. Yet, when viewed alongside other aspects of his personality, this trait hinted at a more profound belief in himself as a paternal figure, not just within his family but extending to all those he interacted with, and indeed to the nation and humanity at large.

This characteristic was particularly pronounced in his involvement with Mrinalini's career. On one level, Vikram could be perceived as a supportive spouse to a working woman.

However, on another level, he seemed to have commandeered her career, incorporating it into a broader project imbued with responsibilities and a social role that Mrinalini had not initially envisaged. This is evident from his detailed response to a BBC question about the formation of Darpana, where he discussed the cultural influences of northern and western India and his admiration for the purity and seriousness of South Indian music and dance. Vikram envisioned establishing a group of dancers and musicians in Gujarat, hoping that over time, a new generation of performers would emerge, thereby enriching the artistic and cultural life of northern India.

In some ways, Vikram's over-involvement in Mrinalini's career mirrored certain traits of his father, Ambalal. For instance, Ambalal's overly serious interpretation of a childhood promise to Vikram regarding a toy in England showcases a similar intensity. However, as Vikram matured, there was a noticeable shift in his demeanour. Those who knew him in later life described him as unpretentious, open-minded and light-hearted, suggesting he had successfully distanced himself from some of the more burdensome aspects of his family's legacy.

This transformation was symbolised by his decision in 1953 to move out of 'The Retreat', the family mansion. While there were practical reasons for this move—Mrinalini's discomfort at 'The Retreat' and possibly Vikram's own sense of constraint—the fact that Vikram did not simply relocate to a nearby independent house or within the estate, unlike many of his siblings, is telling. He was the only one among his siblings, except for Leena, who established an independent home in Ahmedabad outside 'The Retreat's' walls.

Vikram's decision to relocate can be interpreted as a conscious departure from the sheltered life of Ahmedabad's elite, shedding the remnants of feudal attitudes. He chose to establish his new home across the Sabarmati, away from the opulent mansions of

Shahibaug and the dense pols of the old city. In this new setting, amid broad avenues and open spaces, Vikram planted the seeds of his expansive dreams, laying down the building blocks for what would eventually become emblematic of modern Ahmedabad. This move was not just a physical relocation but a metaphorical step towards embracing a more progressive and less constrained way of life.

Vikram's approach to societal change was not one of outright rebellion or alignment with any radical political movements, such as the one advocating for the creation of an ethnically distinct Gujarat. Instead, his strategy was more nuanced and constructive. He aimed to cultivate a new societal class that differed significantly from the traditional entrepreneurial and feudal ethos of Ahmedabad. This emerging class was envisioned as a professionally trained, salaried group, a concept that was somewhat alien to the city's prevailing business culture.

Vikram's initiative to establish this new class was deeply intertwined with his broader social and national objectives. He had already initiated efforts to leverage science and technology for societal advancement, and now he was poised to focus on another area of keen interest: management. His conviction was that management techniques could be harnessed for societal betterment, a belief shared and confirmed by his colleagues, including Jahar Saha, a former director of IIM-A, and MR Kurup.

In India at that time, the concept of professional management was relatively unfamiliar, not only in public enterprises but also in the wider industrial sector. Most businesses were family-owned and traditionally passed down from father to sons. Although some members of business families were starting to seek management education abroad, the idea of formal management training was still relatively new in the country.

Recognising this gap, Vikram, in collaboration with Kasturbhai Lalbhai, took proactive steps in 1956 to address it. Together, they founded the Ahmedabad Management Association (AMA). The AMA was established with the objectives of conducting research and providing training to employees of various companies. Initially operating from a modest room in a bank building, the AMA was destined to expand into a substantial institution. This foundational step laid the groundwork for what would eventually become the prestigious Indian Institute of Management Ahmedabad (IIM-A), a landmark institution in the field of management education in India. Vikram's vision and efforts in establishing the AMA thus marked the beginning of a significant shift in the landscape of professional management education and practice in India, contributing to the growth and development of a new professional class.

During the 1950s, the concept of the Indian Institute of Management Ahmedabad (IIM-A) was still in its nascent stages, more a vague proposal than a concrete plan. The Ford Foundation, established in 1936 by Henry Ford as an independent, non-profit and non-governmental organisation, played a pivotal role in the development of management education in India. Despite some scepticism about the foundation's ties to the US Government, Vikram saw an opportunity in the Ford Foundation's proposal to establish two management institutes in India. Unperturbed by the controversies surrounding the foundation, Vikram, in his characteristic forward-thinking manner, engaged in discussions with his close ally Kasturbhai Lalbhai and Jivraj Mehta, who was soon to become Gujarat's first chief minister. Together, they began advocating for one of these institutes to be established in Ahmedabad.

Vikram envisioned an institution that was modern, professional and cosmopolitan. He had already taken strides towards this vision by implementing merit-based selection criteria at the Physical Research Laboratory (PRL) and ATIRA, attracting talent from across India and fostering a diverse and inclusive environment. However, his ambitions extended beyond national boundaries; he was eager to introduce global perspectives and standards to his peers in Ahmedabad.

S Ramaseshan, reflecting on Vikram's motivations, speculated that his privileged upbringing might have fuelled his desire to elevate others to his level, a sentiment shared by Homi Bhabha. Bhabha, like Vikram, was deeply engaged in establishing public institutions and had successfully invited renowned scientists such as Paul Dirac to India.

Vikram's connections within the international scientific community were extensive. He held significant positions such as secretary of the International Institute Subcommittee on Cosmic Ray Intensity Variations and was a member of the Cosmic Ray Commission of the International Union of Pure and Applied Physics. His network included eminent scientists like Bruno Rossi, James Van Allen (known for discovering the Van Allen radiation belts), Bertrand Goldschmidt, Sydney Chapman, PMS Blackett, Victor Neher and others. PRL hosted visits from illustrious scientists, including Philip Morrison, Alexander J Dessler, Donald A Glaser, Linus Pauling, Y Sekido, Maurice M Shapiro and the Joliot-Curie couple.

Vikram's commitment to international collaboration was unwavering. He actively encouraged students and colleagues to seek training abroad, attend global seminars, and represent India on the world stage. This emphasis on international exposure yielded significant results, exemplified by the work of PRL alumni like Harjit S Ahluwalia, who collaborated with Dessler on a substantial scientific model.

In the late 1950s, an opportunity aligned closely with Vikram's goals emerged: the announcement of the International Geophysical Year (IGY). This event presented a platform for

Vikram to further his agenda of fostering global scientific collaboration and enhancing India's presence in the international scientific community.

The International Geophysical Year (IGY), commencing in July 1957, represented a significant milestone in the annals of scientific history, particularly for its focus on collaborative exploration and research. It was conceived in response to the burgeoning global interest in the potential use of satellites for scientific purposes. The primary aim of the IGY was to conduct a coordinated international study of the Earth's atmosphere and oceans, paving the way for future space exploration. This objective was remarkable, especially considering the prevailing atmosphere of secrecy and nationalism fuelled by World War II and the burgeoning space race between the United States and the Soviet Union. The IGY was characterised by an ethos of shared knowledge pursuit, fostering an unprecedented level of goodwill and cooperation within the international scientific community.

For Vikram and the Physical Research Laboratory (PRL), the IGY presented an ideal platform to engage in this global scientific endeavour. PRL's involvement in the IGY was a natural extension of Vikram's advocacy for international scientific collaboration. Dr KR Ramanathan, the director of PRL and an active member of the national committee of the International Union of Scientific Committees, was appointed by the Indian National Science Academy to lead the Indian National Committee for the IGY, reflecting the institution's prominent role in this international event.

Preparations for the IGY at PRL had started years earlier. Vikram's students, NW Nerurkar and Bhavsar, began developing a cubical meson telescope. The collaboration was further enhanced by the involvement of international experts. Professor Victor Neher from CALTECH (California Institute of Technology) visited as a professor for a year, working alongside PRL's Satya Prakash on neutron monitor components. Upendra

Desai constructed the east-west telescopes, which UR Rao would operate during the IGY.

An interesting episode during this period involved George Clark, a member of Bruno Rossi's team, who visited India in 1955-56 to study cosmic showers near the equator. Vikram escorted him to Kodaikanal, a southern hill station, where one of Vikram's senior students, EV Chitnis, had amassed extensive data on the subject. However, the data's volume was so immense that it couldn't be processed even by the powerful Russian computer at the Indian Statistical Institute in Calcutta. Vikram facilitated the transfer of this data to MIT, which had the latest IBM computer, albeit a tube version occupying an entire basement. Chitnis humorously recalled the IBM computer's frequent malfunctions.

In a significant collaboration during the IGY, PRL partnered with MIT and a Japanese scientific team to establish a large meson monitor at a high-altitude laboratory in Chacaltaya, Bolivia. The data accumulated by PRL from its network of cosmic ray stations across India had become an integral part of the global research network. Vikram's proposal for a worldwide study of cosmic ray variations using standardised equipment was incorporated into the IGY's programme. This period marked a particularly exhilarating phase for the Ahmedabad-based research centre. Vikram, with evident pride, reported the significant contributions of his laboratory to the Cosmic Ray Programme of the IGY at a symposium held at the Tata Institute of Fundamental Research (TIFR) on 23 February 1958, underscoring PRL's vital role in this landmark international scientific initiative.

Vikram Sarabhai's research on cosmic ray variations and the experiments conducted by his students at the Physical Research Laboratory (PRL) were making significant progress in the mid to late 1950s. During this time, an intriguing scientific concept emerged from Eugen N Parker and others regarding the existence of solar wind in interplanetary space.

Parker, a professor at the University of Chicago, introduced the idea of solar wind, a continuous flow of charged particles emitted by the sun, permeating the entire heliosphere. Vikram, who frequently visited the University of Chicago to collaborate with renowned astrophysicist Subramanyan Chandrasekhar and to stay updated on cosmic ray research, likely encountered Parker and his theories during these visits. Vikram's handwritten notes from 1965 to 1971, preserved at the Vikram Sarabhai Archives in Ahmedabad, indicate his keen interest in Parker's hypothesis about solar wind. Motivated by these insights, Vikram initiated experiments at PRL to explore this new avenue of space research.

PMS Blackett, a notable figure in the field, recognised Vikram's substantial contributions to the study of cosmic ray intensity variations. Blackett highlighted Vikram's early understanding of the solar wind's role in the 11-year solar modulation process, the impact of interplanetary magnetic fields, and the significance of gradients in cosmic ray density in interpreting solar daily variations.

Amidst his scientific endeavours and participation in international cosmic ray conferences, Vikram was also deeply involved in managing Sarabhai Chemicals, a business allocated to him from his family's portfolio. Sarabhai Chemicals, part of the Sarabhai Group, was established in the mid-1940s. The company's inception was partly due to the initiative of the ruler of Baroda, who aimed to boost industrial activity in the region by offering industrialists large tracts of barren land at concessional rates. Ambalal Sarabhai, approached by the ruler, acquired fifty acres of land intendingto establish a manufacturing unit for healthcare products. This venture was one of the many dimensions of Vikram Sarabhai's multifaceted career, which encompassed not only groundbreaking scientific research but also significant contributions to industry and entrepreneurship.

The state of the pharmaceutical industry in India during Vikram Sarabhai's tenure at Sarabhai Chemicals was relatively undeveloped, characterised by a lack of advanced technological expertise. This situation necessitated collaborations with international manufacturers to bridge the technological gap. Kasturbhai Lalbhai, entering the pharmaceutical business around the same time, had formed a joint venture with American-based Lederle Laboratories. Similarly, the Sarabhai family opted for a technical collaboration with ER Squibb & Sons, a New York-based company. When Vikram took over as chairman, Sarabhai Chemicals was a modest enterprise, offering a limited range of simple formulations and bulk pharmaceutical chemicals.

Vikram's father, Ambalal Sarabhai, was a trailblazing businessman known for introducing innovative technologies and modern work practices. For instance, the Calico Mills, as noted by VGangadhar, an Ahmedabad-based journalist, was professionally managed with minimal family interference. Although Ambalal's business initiatives were often lauded for their progressiveness, he maintained a distinct separation between his business ventures and his social engagements. Despite his admiration for Mahatma Gandhi and the participation of women in his family in the freedom movement, Ambalal's business decisions remained distinct from his social sympathies.

Vikram, in contrast, achieved a more seamless integration of what might seem like contradictory impulses. This trait was observed and commented upon by various family members. Mrinalini Sarabhai noted that Vikram didn't have the typical divide between private and public personas, maintaining a consistent character in both spheres. Kartikeya Sarabhai echoed this sentiment, emphasising the uniformity of Vikram's motives across different areas of his life. Vikram's personal notes from the late 1960s further illustrate this consistency, as they mirror the points he made in his public speeches, devoid of asides, private reflections, or significant alterations, reflecting a remarkably clear and focused mind.

Vikram inherited not only his ancestors' entrepreneurial spirit and financial acumen—traits Ashis Nandy identified as characteristic of the 'bania' community—but also a pragmatic approach to problem-solving. This practical mindset was evident in his detailed cost-benefit analyses and transparent discussions about financial aspects during job interviews.

However, Vikram's influence extended beyond traditional business practices. He infused his work in research, technology and education with practicality, while bringing innovation and a sense of patriotism to his business ventures. Vikram's holistic approach to his various endeavours, whether in business, science or education, reflected a unique blend of pragmatism, innovation and nationalistic fervour, distinguishing his leadership and vision in each field.

MSSastry's recollection of Vikram Sarabhai's first day at Sarabhai Chemicals vividly illustrates Vikram's meticulous attention to detail and his forward-thinking approach. Vikram's insistence on cleanliness, especially given the nature of the pharmaceutical industry, underscored his commitment to quality and standards. This anecdote also highlights his hands-on approach, as he personally inspected the facility for cleanliness. Furthermore, his meeting with KJ Divatia, a US-trained chemist, reveals Vikram's ambitious vision for Sarabhai Chemicals. His desire to establish a basic industry from scratch was indicative of his entrepreneurial spirit and foresight.

Vikram and Mrinalini's choice of residence also reflected their preference for serene and natural surroundings. They settled in Usmanpura, which at the time was a quiet area on the outskirts of Ahmedabad, where the urban landscape transitioned into rural hinterland. Despite the initial uncleanliness and presence of garbage, the plot's location by the Sabarmati River and its peaceful atmosphere reminded them of their previous home in Malleswaram, leading them to choose it as their new residence.

In designing their new home, named 'Chidambaram' after one of Shiva's dance halls, Vikram enlisted his youngest sister, Gira, who had apprenticed with the renowned American architect Frank Lloyd Wright. The house she designed for them was a blend of contemporary style and comfort, featuring large windows that offered views of the lawns and the river. The interior of the house was a testament to their eclectic tastes, furnished with a mix of Scandinavian-style chairs, bookshelves, large white floor cushions, and an American-style dining section. The decor included raw silk curtains, abstract paintings, modern European ceramics, Japanese drawings, Indian rural pottery and woodwork, creating a space that reflected a blend of different cultures and styles.

Vikram's enthusiasm and dedication to his work were further evident in his weekly trips to the plant in Baroda. The construction of a motorable road between Ahmedabad and Baroda, an event that brought him considerable joy, symbolised the progress and development he valued so highly. Vinodini Mayor's memory of Vikram's excitement about driving by car to Baroda encapsulates his energetic and passionate approach to both his professional and personal endeavours.

Vikram Sarabhai's dynamism and clarity of vision significantly influenced the atmosphere and direction of Sarabhai Chemicals. His assertion of building the industry from scratch resonated with the company's young professionals, inspiring them despite the prevailing industry norm that subsidiaries of multinational pharmaceutical companies were mainly focused on packaging and marketing imported products. Individuals like Divatia and MS Sastry were quickly convinced of Vikram's capabilities and vision, recognising his clear-headed approach from the outset.

However, not everyone at Sarabhai Chemicals was as easily persuaded. The transition of leadership from Ambalal to Vikram, then a young and untested 31-year-old, was met with scepticism by some of the more senior members of the company. Their resistance posed potential challenges to Vikram's ambitious plans. Moreover, navigating relationships with foreign collaborators and dealing with the Indian Government's complex web of regulations and red tape added layers of complexity to his role.

Vikram's previous experience at ATIRA, a research institution run with public funds, was different from managing a private business enterprise. His interest in management as an academic discipline made his approach to these challenges particularly noteworthy. In the initial years, Vikram focused primarily on managing people, an essential aspect considering the landscape of the pharmaceutical business at the time, which was dominated by family-managed companies like Ranbaxy, Cadila and Cipla, and foreign-controlled multinationals such as Glaxo and Pfizer.

Under Vikram's leadership, and likely with Ambalal's endorsement, Sarabhai Chemicals transitioned into a professionally managed company. He restructured the organisation by turning operating and service activities into independent profit centres, each led by chief executives. These CEOs reported to Vikram as chairman, but he also established a supervisory board composed of senior company personnel. This board was given the authority to direct and coordinate the company's affairs, a strategy that effectively mitigated any resentment from older company members.

Vikram's interpersonal skills were also crucial in managing relationships with collaborators. He was known for his charm, which was well-received during his frequent trips to New York. His interactions with JR Geigy, a Swiss company with which he would later sign an agreement, and ER Squibb & Sons, highlighted his diplomatic skills. Squibb, in particular, shared some of Vikram's concerns, such as an intense focus on hygiene, which likely made the collaboration smoother.

Vikram Sarabhai's approach to business management at Sarabhai Chemicals exemplified his ability to blend innovative leadership with practical managerial strategies, fostering a progressive and professionally driven corporate culture in an industry traditionally dominated by family-run businesses and multinational subsidiaries.

The story of Vikram Sarabhai's involvement with Sarabhai Chemicals and his collaboration with international companies like JR Geigy and E Merck highlights his keen attention to detail, innovative approach, and ability to establish and maintain strong professional relationships.

Dr Squibb's reputed practice of personally signing each bottle leaving the company gates reflects a dedication to quality and accountability that resonated with Vikram. While he might have had differences over certain operational aspects, such as housekeeping schedules, Vikram showed considerable respect for the expertise of the professionals sent by these companies. His backing of these experts underscores his commitment to learning from and collaborating with global leaders in the field.

The collaborations with JR Geigy for pharmaceuticals and dyes, and E Merck for vitamin C manufacture, positioned the Sarabhais as pioneers in local bulk drug manufacturing in India. These partnerships were in line with Vikram's vision of backward integration and self-sufficiency in the pharmaceutical industry.

Despite the rapid expansion of the company, Vikram limited his time in Baroda to about a day a week, preferring to delegate responsibilities while maintaining oversight through detailed reports and regular board meetings. His management style emphasised the distinction between abdication and delegation, underscoring the importance of informed leadership.

Vikram's approach to leadership was marked by an intense attention to detail and a personal touch. He was known to engage in casual conversations with colleagues, which could swiftly transition into serious discussions about business challenges, demonstrating his ability to balance light-heartedness with rigorous professional scrutiny. This combination of attentiveness and approachability was appreciated by his staff, who valued his feedback and reactions.

His ability to connect with people was a key factor in his success across various ventures. Descriptions of Vikram's professional relationships often include terms like 'trust', 'mutuality', and 'collaboration', but these words only partially capture the warmth and personal connection he brought to these interactions. The impact of his charm and his capacity to make people feel comfortable and valued was a consistent theme in the recollections of those who worked with him. This personal approach extended beyond mere professional interactions, as he had the unique ability to make individuals feel more complete, responsible and empathetic following their encounters with him.

Vikram Sarabhai's legacy in business and science is marked not just by his achievements and innovations, but also by the profound personal impact he had on those around him, shaping their professional ethos and personal values.

Vikram Sarabhai's leadership and interpersonal style were deeply influenced by both his upbringing and his scientific worldview, setting him apart in his professional and personal interactions.

Ambalal Sarabhai, Vikram's father, was known for his affability and approachability, often sharing meals with employees at the Calico café and engaging in casual conversations about everyday matters like diet and health. Vikram, however, exhibited a more intense and engaging charm. The profound impact he had on those around him is evident in anecdotes about former staffers who treasured his portrait or took his pictures home as a mark of respect and affection. This level of admiration and personal connection is rare and speaks volumes about Vikram's ability to forge deep, meaningful relationships.

Vikram's warmth and friendliness extended to everyone he encountered, regardless of their position. His practice of greeting everyone with equal amiability, from the janitorial staff to senior executives, was a testament to his egalitarian approach. His visits to the workers in the workshop before heading to his office at PRL showcased his genuine interest in the well-being of all members of his team.

His concern for others' personal challenges went beyond mere gestures. Instances like having an employee's quarters repainted to alleviate a spouse's allergy or assisting a colleague in securing a foreign posting for medical treatment demonstrate his empathy and willingness to go above and beyond to support his team. Such acts of kindness were not exceptional events but part of his everyday demeanour.

Vikram's humble and inclusive approach was evident in his interactions with staff and their families, attending their personal events and treating every meeting and summoning with courtesy and respect. As his son Kartikeya noted, Vikram viewed people intrinsically as equals, a perspective that deeply influenced his leadership style.

Vikram's philosophy, as he articulated in a talk, emphasised the importance of leading by example, showcasing creativity, a love of nature, and a dedication to the scientific method. This approach reflects his understanding of the interconnectedness of all organisms, a principle fundamental to science. His belief in the importance of teamwork and collaboration in scientific endeavours was in line with contemporary scientific thought, as highlighted by Werner Von Braun's remarks on the necessity of group expertise in modern science.

Vikram's recognition of the value of every individual, including craftsmen and technicians, in the scientific process was a hallmark of his leadership. His appreciation for skilled craftsmen like Khimjibhai Mistry, who assisted him since childhood and later found a place at PRL, and the glass-blower sent to Manchester for training, underscores his recognition of the essential contributions of all roles in the pursuit of scientific progress. This inclusive and respectful approach to leadership, rooted in both his personal values and his scientific philosophy, set Vikram Sarabhai apart as a visionary leader and a compassionate human being.

Vikram Sarabhai's leadership style was distinct in its focus on building and nurturing teams, a trait that was recognised and admired by contemporaries such as former Prime Minister IK Gujral. This approach was somewhat atypical in the Indian context, where individualism often prevailed. Gujral's observation underscores Vikram's ability to foster collaboration and teamwork, an essential aspect of his success in managing diverse and ambitious projects. While some might argue that this team-building approach was a practical strategy for achieving his goals, it also reflected Vikram's inherent qualities of inclusivity and visionary leadership.

Vikram's management style was influenced by the practices of two individuals he greatly admired: his father, Ambalal Sarabhai, and the renowned physicist Homi Bhabha. Ambalal's strategy of hiring 'gems' or exceptionally talented individuals, and Bhabha's penchant for creating new departments around such talents at the Tata Institute of Fundamental Research (TIFR), inspired Vikram to adopt a similar approach. He recognised the importance of building parts of an institution around key individuals with unique skills and expertise.

An example of Vikram's innovative problem-solving and institutional building was the formation of the Operations

Research Group (ORG), India's first market research agency. This initiative was born out of a conversation with DVN Sarma, a statistician at ATIRA who expressed boredom with his job. Vikram's solution was to create an organisation that would conduct market research, starting with data analysis for the Sarabhai enterprises. The initial experiment of using salesmen from Swastik Oil Mills to track sales data was modest but successful, leading to the expansion of ORG's activities across the country.

Despite his many successes, not all of Vikram's ventures were triumphant. One such example was Limical, a slimming food supplement modelled after the American product Metacal. Vikram, a passionate advocate for health and fitness, was enthusiastic about the product's potential but was disappointed when it did not achieve the expected popularity. Nevertheless, he continued to promote it, even humorously trying to persuade friends and family to try it during breakfast.

Vikram's personal lifestyle reflected his commitment to health and fitness. He was disciplined in his daily routine, performing suryanamaskars (sun salutations) at dawn and maintaining a regular swimming regimen. Despite the variety of dishes available at the Sarabhai family table, he adhered to a simple diet, preferring a single roti with accompaniments like papad, yogurt, mango pickle and salads. His playful habit of nibbling from others' plates, while jesting about calories, was a light-hearted aspect of his personality that his family fondly remembered.

Vikram Sarabhai's blend of visionary leadership, innovative problem-solving, personal discipline, and warmth in personal interactions made him a remarkable figure in both his professional and private life, leaving a lasting impact on those who knew him and on the institutions he helped shape.

By 1956, Vikram Sarabhai had undergone a noticeable physical transformation, developing a more robust and vigorous physique as he approached his forties. This change was complemented by a sense of maturity and an air of vigour, with laughter lines around his eyes indicating a life filled with joy and optimism. Mrinalini Sarabhai's recollections portray him as a person who embraced dreams and possibilities, ready to support and figure out ways to achieve even the most whimsical aspirations.

Vikram's cheerful and spirited nature was reflected in his love for music and singing. He enjoyed songs like the KL Saigal hit Babul mora from the movie Street Singer and was fond of whistling tunes, such as the theme from The Bridge on the River Kwai.This musical inclination was a part of everyday life, as remembered by his daughter Mallika, who recalls marching around with her father whistling tunes.

During this period, Vikram took on the role of a full-time single parent, as Mrinalini was often away for extended periods due to her dance performances and tours, some of which were organised by the Indian Government. Despite the challenges of travel, including modest accommodations and tight budgets, Mrinalini and her dance troupe, Darpana, continued their tours, including an extended trip to Europe.

Vikram's support for Mrinalini extended to regular correspondence, where he would share words of encouragement, updates on their children's health and activities, and expressions of love and affection. His letters often contained vivid descriptions of everyday life at home, reflecting his attentive and nurturing approach as a parent. His commitment to parenting was evident in anecdotes like taking the children shopping during working hours and managing the household in Mrinalini's absence.

The Sarabhai household, 'Chidambaram', was a lively and active place. With multiple cars in the driveway, including a white Sunbeam Talbot with red upholstery, a green Bantam, and a Dodge, and the playful presence of Vikram's dog Sparku and a litter of Siamese cats he had brought for Mallika from Baroda, the home was filled with the hustle and bustle of family life.

Vikram Sarabhai's life at this time paints a picture of a man who successfully balanced his professional responsibilities with a rich and fulfilling personal life, filled with music, love for his family, and an enduring sense of optimism and joy.

The Sarabhai household in 1959 was a vibrant and dynamic place, balancing high-profile social engagements with the joys and challenges of everyday family life. Kartikeya Sarabhai and his friends, including Navroz Contractor, enjoyed the freedom of the expansive lawns, occasionally leading to mishaps like breaking a glass pane while playing, incidents Vikram met with understanding rather than reprimand.

That year, Ahmedabad hosted several distinguished visitors. The Duke of Edinburgh, Prince Philip, arrived at the invitation of the Ahmedabad Management Association, and Mrinalini Sarabhai organised a grand feast in his honour, showcasing her flair for hospitality. The visit of the Rockefellers, Blanchette and John Rockefeller III, also stood out. Mrinalini initially expressed concern that their home, 'Chidambaram', might seem modest for their wealthy American guests. However, Vikram's firm stance that the Rockefellers were coming to see them as they were, not for their home, underscored his confidence in their own identity and lifestyle.

Amidst this backdrop of domestic activity and social engagements, there was the matter of Vikram's relationship with Kamla, a topic that was known but not openly discussed in their social circles. Kamla had made Ahmedabad her home, building a house named 'Avantika' by the river. The relationship between Vikram and Kamla, strengthened by their shared interest in professional management, was an open secret. Prakash Tandon described their compatibility and professional rapport, noting their complementary personalities and shared focus on human relations and management.

The affair between Vikram and Kamla did not seem to cause significant scandal, likely due to the Sarabhais' reputation for eccentricity and a liberal approach to personal relationships. Vikram's aunt Ansuya, brother Gautam, and his partner Kamlini Khatau were known for their progressive views, reflecting a family ethos of individual freedom and broad-mindedness. This attitude of permissiveness and perhaps a degree of indifference within the Sarabhai family likely contributed to the acceptance, or at least the lack of overt judgement, regarding Vikram's relationship with Kamla.

The unique dynamics of Vikram Sarabhai's personal life, particularly his relationships with Mrinalini and Kamla, reflected his unconventional approach to morality and human relationships. Vikram's views on morality were influenced by his understanding of the Upanishads and the concept of relativity, leading him to question absolute notions of right and wrong. This philosophical stance seemed to shape the way he navigated his personal relationships, creating a somewhat unconventional and complex situation.

Despite his relationship with Kamla, Vikram continued to hold deep admiration and affection for Mrinalini, his wife. Interestingly, this situation did not provoke the expected reactions, given Mrinalini's bold and outspoken nature. The three maintained a social circle with an air of friendly exuberance, indicative of a light-hearted, albeit unconventional, approach to their relationships. However, this seemingly carefree dynamic was not sustainable, and Vikram's underestimation of the potential emotional impact on Mrinalini suggested a blind spot in his otherwise complex and reasoned thinking.

Amidst these personal developments, Vikram faced challenges in realising his vision for a world-class management institute in Ahmedabad. The initial feedback from a team of researchers sent by the Ford Foundation was discouraging, as they believed India's priority should be primary education due to widespread poverty. Undeterred, Vikram successfully advocated for a second team to evaluate the proposal, which resulted in a more favourable opinion. This positive second assessment paved the way for Vikram to seek collaboration with Harvard University for the project.

The Indian Institute of Management Ahmedabad (IIM-A) was a dream shared by Vikram and Kamla, and both were deeply involved in its conceptualisation and realisation. Prakash Tandon, with his Harvard background and friendship with Vikram, became a valuable contributor to this endeavour.

Meanwhile, the sociopolitical landscape in Ahmedabad and Gujarat was undergoing significant changes. The establishment of an independent Gujarat state had ignited parochial sentiments, particularly regarding language policy in education. The debate centred on the role of English in schools, with local politicians advocating for its introduction at a later stage in the curriculum, reflecting a preference for native languages in early education.

Vikram Sarabhai's foray into the political arena of educational policy-making, particularly his involvement in the vice-chancellor elections at Gujarat University, highlights his deep commitment to modernising education and his willingness to step outside his comfort zone to advocate for his beliefs.

As the head of the Physical Research Laboratory (PRL), Vikram was part of the decision-making apparatus of Gujarat University. His stance on modernising higher education, especially his support for the early teaching of English in schools, was in stark contrast to the prevailing parochial views of local leaders. Concerned about the potential impact of these parochial views on the future employability and educational opportunities for Gujaratis, Vikram made the bold decision to run for the position of vice-chancellor.

The election for vice-chancellor was a challenging battleground for Vikram. Despite his reputation, influence from his prominent family, and significant contributions to the city through various institutions, he faced formidable opposition. His lack of experience in the politically charged and complex environment of university governance was a significant handicap.

Vikram's decision to engage in this battle seems, in retrospect, to be a venture far outside his usual realm of expertise. Umashanker Joshi's observation that Vikram might have been frustrated with the university's direction and wanted to bring focus to his views, even if it meant facing failure, sheds light on his motivations. Alternatively, it is possible that Vikram underestimated the opposition he would face.

The political landscape of Gujarat's academic world at that time was heavily influenced by caste dynamics and was dominated by the Congress Party's upper-caste Brahmin clique, led by figures such as Morarji Desai. The election was not just a matter of policy but also a matter of prestige for them. Against this backdrop, Vikram, even with the support of influential figures like Kasturbhai Lalbhai, faced an uphill battle. The seasoned politicians dismissed him as an 'establishment man' and a 'representative of the mill owners', and they exerted considerable influence over senate members.

Ultimately, Vikram lost the election to Lalbhai Desai, a retired school inspector. This episode in Vikram's life illustrates his commitment to educational reform and his willingness to engage in unfamiliar and challenging arenas to advocate for his vision. Despite the setback, this experience underscores Vikram's multifaceted personality and his dedication to causes he believed were essential for the progress and modernisation of education in his region.

Vikram Sarabhai's response to his defeat in the vice-chancellor election at Gujarat University, as recounted by V Gangadhar and others, exemplifies his philosophical outlook and ability to maintain objectivity. Drawing inspiration from the Bhagavad Gita, he likely viewed the experience as part of the larger journey, rather than a setback. His son Kartikeya's reflection suggests that Vikram may have learned from this episode the importance of not being confined to a specific position to effect change.

This perspective was validated when Harvard University agreed to Vikram's proposal, leading to the establishment of the Indian Institute of Management Ahmedabad (IIM-A) in 1962. This achievement underscored Vikram's ability to realise his visions through persistence and strategic thinking, independent of holding a formal position of authority.

At Sarabhai Chemicals, Vikram's unconventional management style often surprised his executives. They were accustomed to his sudden inspirations, like the strategic purchase of land in Ankleshwar anticipating its development into a petrochemical hub. His attention to detail was such that an employee had to cancel a vacation over a quality control issue. His approach to business was not just about maintaining high standards but also about fostering competition and innovation.

The success of the Operations Research Group (ORG) is a testament to Vikram's foresight. Rather than keeping ORG solely for the benefit of Sarabhai Chemicals, he advocated for it to operate as a separate profit centre, selling its services in the open market. This decision was grounded in his belief in the importance of competition and providing equal opportunities to all players in the market.

Vikram applied the same principles to other ventures, such as the Sarabhai Research Centre and Sarabhai Glass. These initiatives were not just business enterprises but part of his larger goal to establish a foundational industry in India. His insistence on selling products in the open market, even to competitors, was initially met with scepticism by colleagues like KJ Divatia. However, this approach ultimately proved to be visionary, as it fostered a competitive and dynamic business environment.

Vikram Sarabhai's journey in establishing a basic industry from scratch and his progressive approach to business management highlight his innovative spirit and commitment to creating an equitable and competitive industrial landscape in India. His ability to balance ambitious undertakings, like the production of antibiotics, with his philosophical and egalitarian approach to business, demonstrates the depth and breadth of his impact as a leader and visionary.

Vikram Sarabhai's strategic moves in the pharmaceutical industry and his significant role in the establishment of the Indian Institute of Management Ahmedabad (IIM-A) illustrate his multifaceted vision and innovative approach.

In the pharmaceutical sector, Vikram recognised the importance of India producing its own bulk drugs like penicillin and streptomycin. Facing governmental restrictions on licensing in this area, he cleverly navigated these challenges by purchasing Standard Pharmaceuticals in Kolkata, which already had a licence to produce penicillin. This move, while resourceful, marked the beginning of a prolonged struggle to acquire the necessary foreign exchange for importing machinery, reflecting his determination to develop this crucial industry domestically.

Concurrently, Vikram was instrumental in shaping IIM-A. Along with Kasturbhai Lalbhai, who managed the project, he played a key role in its development. Vikram's suggestion to involve the internationally acclaimed architect Louis Kahn in designing the IIM-A campus showcased his interest in architecture and his commitment to creating an inspiring educational environment. This interest was also evident in his collaborations with local architects like Balkrishna Doshi and in the design of other institutions he was involved with, such as the Darpana Academy of Performing Arts.

While IIM-A's permanent campus was under construction, the institute temporarily operated from a bungalow in Shahibaug. Kamla, the first senior professor at IIM-A, furthered her expertise by attending Harvard's advanced management programme, underscoring the Sarabhais' commitment to integrating world-class educational practices into IIM-A.

Vikram's choice of Harvard Business School as a model for IIM-A was not just about adopting an established educational partner but also embracing a specific educational philosophy. The Harvard case study method, implemented at IIM-A, was more than a teaching tool; it represented a paradigm shift in bringing real-world experiences into the classroom. This approach influenced various aspects of IIM-A's functioning, from emphasising functional areas of management education to recruiting a blend of academicians and practitioners and fostering a collaborative culture among the faculty.

The impact of Vikram and Kamla Sarabhai on IIM-A extended beyond the institute's structure and curriculum. They were instrumental in developing processes and systems that ensured the organisational viability of the institute, contributing significantly to its growth and relevance in various sectors of national importance, including banking, agriculture, government systems and education.

During this period, Vikram Sarabhai was deeply involved in a range of ambitious projects, reflecting his diverse interests and commitment to both scientific research and the development of educational and cultural institutions in India.

His approach to training at the Indian Institute of Management Ahmedabad (IIM-A) was innovative, as seen in the decision to send newly recruited faculty members to the Harvard Business School's teacher training programme. This initiative reflected his commitment to excellence and coherence in educational philosophy. Vikram's personal involvement and support for his staff, such as approving funds for the development of Indian case studies and hosting informal gatherings, demonstrated his hands-on leadership style.

At the same time, Vikram faced challenges in his endeavours in the pharmaceutical industry. Despite governmental restrictions, he pursued the production of bulk drugs in India, showcasing his resourcefulness and determination. Meanwhile, he was also involved in the global scientific community, discussing significant topics such as atomic power and participating in conferences like the Pugwash Movement.

The backdrop of political and military tensions, such as the 1962 Sino-Indian War, added complexity to this period. Vikram's travels and conversations during this time, including with Erik Erikson, touched upon these global issues, showing his engagement with current affairs and their impact on India.

Amidst these developments, Vikram played a role in the founding of the National Institute of Design (NID) in Ahmedabad. Initiated by Pupul Jayakar and supported by the Sarabhai family, NID was set up with the help of influential figures like Charles Eames. Vikram, though not primarily focused on design, contributed to the project, underscoring his appreciation for aesthetics and his ability to mobilise support for new initiatives.

Despite his extensive travels and involvement in various projects, Vikram remained committed to his scientific work. His handwritten notes from different locations around the world indicate that physics and scientific inquiry were always at the forefront of his mind. This period in Vikram Sarabhai's life highlights his remarkable ability to balance and excel in multiple roles, from scientific research and educational leadership to cultural development and international diplomacy. His contributions during this time had a lasting impact on various fields, both in India and globally.

❑

Venture into Space

In the 1950s, the concept of a rocket-launching programme was already taking shape, with its origins tracing back to the early part of the decade. Praful Bhavsar, who temporarily left the Physical Research Laboratory (PRL) for post-doctoral work at the University of Minnesota, fondly remembers a conversation with Vikram in 1959. Vikram shared his vision of a future rocket programme and expressed his wish for Bhavsar to return to India to contribute to this ambitious endeavour.

This idea of space exploration wasn't entirely new. In 1865, Jules Verne's novel From the Earth to the Moon depicted a journey to the moon using an artillery shell, capturing the imaginations of many. HG Wells's 1898 novel The War of the Worlds further stirred public interest with its portrayal of a Martian invasion of Earth. Additionally, Konstantin E Tsiolkovsky, a Russian physics teacher, had already conceptualised the idea of spacecraftand rockets powered by liquid hydrogen. These imaginative works likely influenced Vikram, who lived in an era when rocketry was evolving rapidly, making the prospect of actual space exploration increasingly feasible.

The launch of Sputnik 1 by the Soviet Union on 4 October 1957, marked a significant milestone in space exploration, sparking intense competition, particularly in the United States. The US rapidly mobilised its resources, including talent from abroad like Werner Von Braun, to surpass its communist rival in the space race. Meanwhile, Vikram was laying the groundwork for what appeared to be a long-considered plan for India's entry into space exploration.

The exact time when Vikram first envisioned an Indian space programme remains uncertain. His former student, RG Rastogi, recalls Vikram speaking about establishing such a programme. Bhavsar even shared details of this conversation with Professor Jacques E Blamont of the University of Paris during Blamont's visit to Minnesota. Intrigued, Blamont, who had recently started the French Space Research Programme, planned to meet Vikram at the first space science symposium of the Committee for Space Research (COSPAR) in Nice in January 1960. Their meeting indeed took place, leading to a lasting friendship. Blamont's visit to India in November 1963 and his participation in a seminar in Kodaikanal in January 1965, alongside other notable figures like Sydney ABowhill, further cemented this international collaboration.

Given Vikram's keen interest in rockets and his international exposure, it was evident that he aspired to utilise rockets for space experiments. Yet, at that time, even the idea of a modest rocket programme, let alone a comprehensive one involving artificial satellites and launchers, which Vikram would gradually develop, seemed quite bold and ambitious.

Rastogi highlighted a significant scepticism within the Physical Research Laboratory (PRL) regarding Vikram's ambitious plans for a space programme. KR Ramanathan, Vikram's co-director at PRL, doubted Vikram's prospects, citing his youth and inexperience with government operations. Ramanathan believed that Vikram would struggle to secure funding and face resistance from established scientists.

However, Ramanathan underestimated Vikram's connection with Homi J Bhabha, a key figure in Indian science. There's a romantic notion that Vikram and Bhabha, during their younger days in Bangalore, might have dreamt up future scientific endeavours together. Whether discussing ambitious plans at the Indian Institute of Science or making lifelong commitments, there was a sense of destiny in their actions and decisions.

In August 1961, influenced by Bhabha, the Indian Government recognised 'space research and the peaceful uses of outer space' as important areas, placing them under the Department of Atomic Energy (DAE). The PRL was designated as the central hub for space science research and development, and Vikram was appointed to the Atomic Energy Commission (AEC) board. By February 1962, the DAE established the Indian National Committee for Space Research (INCOSPAR) under Vikram's leadership, marking his significant progress in overcoming initial obstacles.

The next challenge was to locate a suitable site for a sounding rocket programme. Sounding rockets, similar to large firecrackers, were used for high-altitude experimental tests. These rockets, equipped with telemetry systems for tracking and sometimes sophisticated sensors, were crucial for scientists and space technologists alike. They offered a foundational understanding of technologies needed for launching orbiting satellites.

Considering the risks of falling debris, the location for the sounding rocket programme had to be isolated and ideally near the magnetic equator. EV Chitnis, one of Vikram's earliest students, was tasked with finding this site.

The launch of Sputnik 1 and the ensuing space race indirectly benefited the PRL. By the late 1950s, many of Vikram's students had completed their doctorates and were welcomed into American laboratories, reflecting the international recognition of their talents. Bhavsar joined the University of Minnesota, Chitnis went to MIT, and UR Rao collaborated with Minoru Oda, a Japanese scientist known for his work in X-ray astronomy. This global outreach and recognition laid a solid foundation for India's foray into space research and exploration.

In July 1962, EV Chitnis, serving as the member-secretary of INCOSPAR, embarked on an extensive survey of India's southern coast to identify a suitable location for a sounding rocket programme. His journey involved nearly two hundred flights in a Dakota, often navigating through monsoon clouds, before narrowing down three potential sites. Later in November, Bhabha and Vikram personally visited these locations to make the final decision.

A photograph from this mission captures a moment during their exploration: Bhabha, slightly portly and wearing thick glasses, dressed in a short-sleeved safari suit, pointing into the distance. Beside him, Vikram, in rolled-up shirt sleeves and light trousers, is seen following Bhabha's gesture. In the background, tall palm trees stretch into the clear sky.

Their journey to the sites was eventful. Despite Chitnis' request, Bhabha couldn't sit in the co-pilot's seat, so they flew low over the lush coastline between Trivandrum and Alleppey. Upon landing at Trivandrum airport, a convoy of large American cars transported them to the sites under consideration. After two days of exploring the humid landscape, they discarded Vellana Thuruthu, due to concerns about it becoming a national joke.

During a dinner invitation at Raj Bhavan by VV Giri, then the governor of Kerala, Chitnis remembered Vikram charmingly mingling with guests after a quick grooming session, demonstrating his ease in social settings.

Ultimately, Thumba, a picturesque fishing village near Trivandrum, was chosen for its strategic advantages, including proximity to the airport and a sparse population. The decision was also influenced by the support of two influential local figures: Bishop Peter Bernard Pereira and the collector, Madhavan Nair. They played a crucial role in peacefully relocating the fishermen to newly built accommodations.

For the development of both a rocket-launching site and a research centre, the selected area encompassed a beach and a hill behind it. RD John from the Central Public Works Department, involved in the project, noted Vikram's cautious approach in land acquisition and planning for the main building, which initially was to accommodate only 200 people. However, Bhabha advised planning for a larger capacity of 400 and insisted on air-conditioning due to the humidity.

Simultaneously, Vikram focused on assembling a team for the upcoming programme. An advertisement in an Indian embassy publication in WashingtonDC, attracted several Indian professionals from NASA and American universities, including PRL alumni and individuals from the atomic energy programme. Among the notable recruits was a young Muslim man from Tamil Nadu, discovered by MGK Menon of TIFR at a defence laboratory in Bangalore. This young man's potential was evident during his interview with Vikram in Bombay, marking another step forward in India's burgeoning space programme.

APJ Abdul Kalam, who later became the head of India's missile development programme and the president of India, detailed his initial meeting with Dr Vikram Sarabhai in his autobiography Wings of Fire. He fondly recalled Dr Sarabhai's warmth and lack of arrogance, which is often seen in interviewers when they interact with young candidates. Dr Sarabhai's approach was not to assess Kalam's current knowledge or skills but to explore the potential and possibilities he embodied. Kalam felt that this encounter was a moment of truth, where his personal dream was embraced and expanded by the larger vision of Dr Sarabhai.

Similarly, Dr K Kasturirangan, who would later serve as the chairman of the Space Commission and Secretary of the Department of Space in the Indian Government from 1994 to 2003, shared his experience of applying to PRL in July 1963. Dr Sarabhai's initial remark about the modest pay and suggestionof a career in banking was a test of Kasturirangan's commitment to science. Once convinced of Kasturirangan's determination, Dr Sarabhai shared his vision for space exploration, all within a concise 15-minute conversation. This interaction showcased Dr Sarabhai'shumane nature, his grasp of practical realities, and his visionary outlook.

For the burgeoning space programme, Vikram selected a group of talented young individuals to be sent to NASA for training at the Goddard Space Flight Centre and the Wallops Island facility. This decision aligned with the spirit of global cooperation that had emerged with the International Geophysical Year (IGY). The United States, recognising the value of this collaboration, offered substantial support.

Both the United Nations Committee on the Peaceful Uses of Outer Space and COSPAR (Committee for Space Research) highlighted the importance of establishing a sounding rocket launch station near the magnetic equator. This was to address gaps in understanding the 'equatorial electrojet', a stream of electric currents near the equator. Praful Bhavsar remembered Jacques E Blamont's enthusiasm for this project, envisioning a launch range at the equator to showcase the majestic trails of rockets to the world. The international scientific community was supportive of India's initiative in this domain. The French space agency, CNES, provided a radar system, the Russians contributed a Minsk computer, and the Americans promised training and additional support, marking a significant collaboration in the field of space research and exploration.

On 21 November 1963, India was poised to launch its first rocket, marking a significant milestone in its space exploration journey. The event drew a gathering of prominent figures from the world of science and technology. Jacques E Blamont, along with his assistants Mary Lise Channin and Michel Autier from France, observers from Brazil and Argentina, and representatives from NASA including Arnold Frutkin, Robert Duffy and Ed Bissel, were present. The Indian contingent was equally distinguished, featuring Homi J Bhabha, Dr AP Mitra from the National Physical Laboratory, and Dr PR Pisharoty, founder director of the Indian Institute of Tropical Meteorology in Poona. The governor of Kerala, the district collector, and the bishop also attended.

This momentous occasion was set against a backdrop of stunning natural beauty, with gentle waves under the sun and trees reaching up into the azure sky. Despite the picturesque setting, there was palpable tension among the Indian attendees, stemming from a series of challenges leading up to the launch.

Several mishaps had already occurred. The Nike-Apache rocket, supplied by NASA, was flown to Delhi but encountered problems during transport to Cochin, leaving it stranded en route. Once this issue was resolved, a new problem emerged: the French payload intended for atmospheric release couldn't fit into the American rocket. Ratilal Panchal, PRL's expert mechanic, had to be flown in from Ahmedabad. With supervision from Praful Bhavsar and APJ Abdul Kalam, Panchal manually adjusted the payload.

Additionally, camera assistants positioned at Kanyakumari, Palayamkottai, Kodaikanal and Kottayam were trained to photograph the cloud released by the rocket. However, there were concerns about potential phone line failures disrupting communication and unfavourable weather conditions affecting the quality of the images.

On the day of the launch, as the rocket was being moved to the launch pad, the atmosphere was charged with tension. A hydraulic leak in the crane's system while hoisting the rocket onto the launcher added to the stress, requiring technicians to move the rocket manually. Further complications arose with the remote system used to adjust the launcher's angle, leading to manual operation.

Finally, after resolving these issues, the area around the launch pad was cleared, and the team anxiously awaited the launch. In a dramatic turn of events, Pramod Kale, a new student at PRL, noticed a worker still tampering with the launcher controls and intervened just in time.

At 6:25 p.m., the rocket was successfully launched into the dusk sky. Minutes later, the sodium vapour payload, illuminated by the setting sun, created a stunning orange cloud high above, symbolising a triumphant moment in India's space exploration history.

RD John vividly remembered the exhilaration at the moment of the rocket's successful launch. In the oval canteen, everyone, including Bhabha, was overwhelmed with joy. Vikram's telegram, succinctly expressing his excitement with the words 'Gee whiz wonderful rocket shot', encapsulated the triumphant mood of the occasion.

Historically, rockets were predominantly used for military purposes. Their use dates back to the 13th century in China and the 18th century by Tipu Sultan against the British. The 19th and 20th centuries saw the Russians, Americans, and Germans enter the field, with their efforts largely driven by aggressive motives. Even scientific studies on rockets during the 1940s and 1950s were often tied to military applications, such as investigating atmospheric effects on radio communications or exploring solar guidance systems for missiles. The Cold War further accelerated the US space effort, fostering advancements in artificial satellite design and missile technology.

In stark contrast, the Indian space programme from its inception focused on peaceful applications. Sounding rockets, for example, were utilised for space science to gather data on atmospheric phenomena like wind velocities and turbulence in the 80-180 kilometre altitude range. For a country like India, which was then considered technologically backward, even a modest-sounding rocket programme was a bold venture. However, Vikram's vision extended far beyond, both in scale and urgency. As Kalam noted, Vikram wasted no time after the launch of the Nike-Apache rocket to discuss his ambition for an Indian satellite launch vehicle.

The purpose of satellites in the Indian context became clearer during a space science seminar organised by PRL in January 1963. Just before the seminar, Bhabha, upon asking Vikram what he should announce, was instructed to declare India's intent to develop satellites for communications. This statement was particularly bold considering the global context: the Soviet Union had just launched the world's first early bird or synchronous satellite, and satellite technology seemed exclusive to wealthy nations.

Throughout the late 1960s, Vikram consistently revealed ambitious plans for space technology in his papers and speeches. These plans caught international attention and admiration, notably from the esteemed Japanese space scientist Hideo Itokawa. Vikram's primary focus, though, remained on national needs. He envisioned space technology playing a crucial role in long-range weather forecasting, a vital application for India. Vikram's perspective on the interconnectedness of natural phenomena—the sun's influence on weather, rivers, vegetation, fossil fuels, life and even communication—underscored the depth and breadth of his vision. His belief in space exploration as a powerful tool for understanding these links exemplified a forward-thinking approach, combining scientific curiosity with practical applications for the betterment of society.

By 1970, Vikram Sarabhai's vision for the Indian space programme had evolved to encompass a broad range of applications, including agriculture, forestry, oceanography, geology, mineral prospecting and cartography. But beyond these specific applications, he believed in the intrinsic benefits of having a space programme itself. In his 1966 paper, 'Space Activity for Developing Countries', published in the science and technology series of the American Astronautical Society of California, he discussed the space programme's potential to stimulate growth in advanced fields such as electronics, chemicals, cybernetics, and materials engineering. He also highlighted the possibility of establishing collaborative relationships with international organisations, scientists, and technologists, and importantly, fostering a culture where people from diverse activities could unite towards a singular objective.

Vikram's dream was to intertwine technology with development, aiming to meet the needs of the masses while promoting a sophisticated work culture and scientific capabilities. He often used the term 'leapfrogging' to describe his belief, shared with Homi J Bhabha and Jawaharlal Nehru, in technology's power to enable developing countries to bypass the lengthy developmental processes experienced by Western countries. He argued against the notion that developing nations should follow the same step-by-step process as advanced nations, emphasising the need for the most effective means to address significant problems.

Vikram also occasionally critiqued the perceived follies of the developed world. In a broadcast talk in 1966 titled 'Sources of Man's Knowledge', he stated that India's immediate goals in space research were modest, humorously dismissing ambitions like sending a man to the moon or orbiting elephants of any colour around Earth. This comment was a subtle jibe at the space race between the US and the Soviet Union, who were then competitively demonstrating their space capabilities.

However, his remark about 'pink elephants' was not just facetious; it reflected a deeper concern about the potential diversion of the space programme from its intended social goals. He warned of the real danger that developing nations might pursue space programmes for their glamour, using resources not for the recognised values of space technology but rather to create a superficial national and international image. This perspective underscored Vikram's commitment to ensuring that India's space endeavours remained focused on practical and socially beneficial applications, rather than merely seeking to compete in the global space race.

Vikram Sarabhai's vision for India's space programme was focused and clear: to develop a space programme that would not only advance scientific research but also offer applications with significant social and economic benefits. Remarkably, Vikram maintained this focus on peaceful purposes, which is particularly notable considering the usual military orientation of many early space programmes worldwide. This commitment to peaceful applications was even more striking given the dual-purpose nature of the Department of Atomic Energy (DAE)—energy and security—under which the space programme was initially established.

Vikram was well aware of the military potential of the technology he was developing. Vasant Gowarikar, who joined the programme in the late 1960s, acknowledged that Vikram was fully cognizant of the defence applications, including Intercontinental Ballistic Missile (ICBM) technology. An incident recounted by journalist Raj Chengappa illustrates this awareness. During a meeting of the Electronics Committee led by Homi J Bhabha in November 1962, amidst discussions following the Chinese invasion, Group Captain VS Narayanan spoke about the need for a radar system capable of detecting ballistic missiles and aircraft and the importance of having a deterrent in the form of ballistic missiles. Vikram, rather than being offended by these remarks, engaged Narayanan in further discussion.

Despite his understanding of the security concerns and the military potential of space technology, Vikram never allowed these aspects to shift the priorities of the space programme. The development of missiles was later undertaken by the Defence Research and Development Organisation (DRDO), separate from the space programme. However, the communication lines between the space programme and defence sectors were open. As Pramod Kale noted, while the space programme was dedicated to peaceful purposes, the capabilities developed could be of assistance if the government required them, indicating a collaborative but distinct relationship between the space and defence sectors.

The establishment of the sounding rocket programme, a time-consuming endeavour, did not hinder Vikram's scientific pursuits or those of his colleagues. Scientists like KG McCracken from MIT and UR Rao continued their meticulous research, including studying the effects of geomagnetic bending on cosmic ray particles arriving on Earth. Other students engaged in experiments to gather data on the Earth's magnetic field and plasma parameters in interplanetary space. This continued dedication to scientific exploration underlined Vikram's commitment to using space technology for peaceful, scientific, and socially beneficial purposes.

The early days of India's space programme involved a mix of successful and unsuccessful experiments, some of which were carried out using balloons or rockets. Dr K Kasturirangan, reflecting on this period, recalled Vikram Sarabhai's response to a series of failed attempts, humorously inquiring if the 'Spanish armada' had returned. Vikram's approach was not only light-hearted but also educational; he emphasised learning from failures by establishing review systems and encouraged risk-taking, a practice that later benefited those who assumed leadership roles.

At the Physical Research Laboratory (PRL), activity was bustling. Vikram had introduced an informal practice common in Western universities: faculty gatherings over morning tea. These sessions provided opportunities for casual conversations, exchange of jokes, and discussions on topics like cricket scores, alongside the scientific dialogue. This environment fostered a sense of community and encouraged open communication among colleagues.

Simultaneously, Vikram, wearing his businessman hat, was engaged in a challenging battle with the government. Like many Indian entrepreneurs during the early years of independence, he faced discouragement and bureaucratic hurdles. Prakash Tandon's book vividly describes the frustration of dealing with the government, emphasising the anxieties and setbacks that businesspeople frequently encounter.

The Sarabhais' struggles included a stand-off with the central government over permission to manufacture antibiotics. KJ Divatia recalled these meetings as frustrating, marked by intense discussions and disagreements with officials like the then minister for industries, Manubhai Shah. Despite the challenges, Vikram remained composed and patient, consistently expressing gratitude in his correspondence with the government, even when following up on applications pending for years.

GD Zalani, appointed as the liaison for the Sarabhais in Delhi, observed that Vikram typically delegated interactions with bureaucrats to his CEOs, reserving his involvement for matters of significant importance. Despite the need for frequent visits to Delhi, Vikram maintained a light-hearted demeanour. Zalani shared anecdotes of Vikram's unique requests and situations, like unexpectedly wanting idli for breakfast, showcasing Vikram's personal side amidst his professional endeavours.

These anecdotes paint a picture of Vikram Sarabhai as a multifaceted individual, balancing his roles as a scientist and an entrepreneur, while fostering a collaborative and innovative culture at PRL and navigating the complexities of Indian bureaucracy with patience and determination.

While in Delhi, Vikram Sarabhai consistently chose to stay at the Ashoka Hotel, a government-owned establishment that, despite not being as luxurious as the privately-run Oberoi, was centrally located and favoured by the Sarabhais. He was regularly accommodated in room number 30, a suite with both a sitting room and bedroom, reserved for him at a special concessional rate. This arrangement reflected his preference for convenience and familiarity over luxury.

Vikram's pace of life was notably brisk, often to the exasperation of those around him. He was known for urging his company driver, Babulal, to exceed his instructed speed limit of 40 km/h due to his invariably tight schedule. GD Zalani, in particular, recalled the stress of dealing with Vikram's last-minute arrivals for flights and the challenges of keeping up with his energetic pace.

Despite his casual approach to personal matters, such as frequently forgetting personal items or dressing simply in light cotton shirts, trousers, or khadi suits (often paired with Kolhapuri chappals due to a foot condition), Vikram maintained high standards for his executives' appearance and engagement with new developments in their work areas.

Vikram's personality was a blend of eccentricity, humour, and optimism. He was appreciated for his 'puckish sense of humour' and his ability to simultaneously engage with multiple subjects, which he found more relaxing than focusing on a single topic for too long. NR Nadkarni, a former director of the Sarabhai Group of companies, highlighted Vikram's unique ability to switch topics and handle various matters concurrently, a trait he described as having a 'multi-channel brain'.

An interesting habit of Vikram's, which he found rejuvenating, was taking short naps after lunch. Nadkarni shared an anecdote about a trip from New Brunswick to New York, during which Vikram, amid a conversation, took a brief nap in the car and woke up completely refreshed to resume the discussion.

Regarding his struggles with the government over obtaining foreign exchange for penicillin production machinery, Vikram eventually conceded. Unable to secure the necessary support, he entered into a collaboration with Squibb, a compromise that, while not ideal, was a practical solution under the circumstances. This situation illustrates Vikram's pragmatic approach to balancing his scientific aspirations with the realities of doing business in the context of Indian bureaucracy and policy constraints.

Kartikeya Sarabhai, reflecting on his father Vikram Sarabhai's life, recounted a conversation with TN Seshan, India's former election commissioner, who had worked closely with Vikram. Seshan's question about whether Vikram considered himself infallible highlighted a crucial aspect of Vikram's personality. Those who knew him well acknowledged him as a loving and sensitive individual, with an innate ability to inspire people to offer their best, as noted by Kamal Mangaldas.

However, Vikram's work ethic was exceptionally demanding. He was known for his early starts, working tirelessly into the night, and maintaining a hectic travel schedule at a time when air travel in India was limited and often disrupted. He viewed time as flexible, much like a 'rubber band', and would engage in discussions with his children about his frequent absences, which they highlighted through a calendar marked with coloured squares for the days he was home.

Kartikeya recalled instances from his childhood when Vikram would break promises due to work commitments, like missing planned swimming trips. The intensity of Vikram's professional life, encompassing vast responsibilities and a wide range of involvements, was overwhelming even for his colleagues. Seshan once missed an early flight due to exhaustion, and Vikram's personal assistant, NVG Warrier, nearly collapsed at an airport, indicating the immense pressure and pace Vikram set for himself and those around him.

Vikram's approach to personal relationships also mirrored this complexity. He managed to juggle multiple professional roles successfully, seemingly applying the same principle to his personal life. He maintained relationships with both his wife and mistress, leading dual lives without contemplating choosing between them. According to Kamla, Vikram's wife, the topic of divorce was never considered, nor would she have preferred it. Mrinalini, Vikram's mistress, expressed her deep love for him, revealing that Vikram wanted her to feel integrated into the family, a situation she tried to accommodate, though not without difficulty.

This portrayal of Vikram Sarabhai reveals a man of extraordinary capabilities and complexities, balancing immense professional responsibilities with intricate personal relationships, often pushing the boundaries of what was conventionally expected or accepted.

Vikram Sarabhai's attempt to reconcile the complexities of his personal life reflects the multifaceted nature of his character and the challenges he faced. His efforts to maintain relationships with both his wife Kamla and his mistress Mrinalini without causing hurt to either indicate his struggle with the impracticality of his expectations. Vikram seemed genuinely surprised and pained to see Mrinalini distressed by the situation, as Mallika, his daughter, vividly recounted.

In his letter to Mrinalini, Vikram expressed deep affection and a longing for understanding, acknowledging his faults and affirming his love for her as both a mother and a woman. This correspondence underscores his desire for a sincere connection amidst the complicated dynamics of his relationships.

Simultaneously, Vikram faced professional dilemmas, particularly regarding the succession for the director's position at the Indian Institute of Management Ahmedabad (IIM-A). Kamla, as the institute's most senior professor and acting director, was a logical successor. However, objections from Harvard, which perceived her as not firm enough, and the ensuing controversy affected both Vikram and Kamla. Vikram, feeling that he had let Kamla down by not resigning from the board, experienced significant distress over the situation.

His anguish was evident in his communication with Mrinalini, where he expressed a sense of guilt for unintentionally hurting those he loved, leading to doubts about the sincerity of his affections. This internal conflict highlighted a deep sense of responsibility and the burden of his decisions on his personal relationships.

Vikram's upbringing and personal ethos, which emphasised self-reliance and strength, hindered his ability to seek support or express doubts. Mallika noted that this code of self-reliance prevented him from showing vulnerability, perceived as a flaw in character. Consequently, Vikram found it challenging to confide in others or establish intimate connections, leading to a sense of isolation in times of turmoil.

In his search for solace, Vikram turned to a Gandhian approach of self-punishment and introspection. His retreat to 'Ghoghu', a glass-fronted hut by the river bank built by his nephew Kamal, became a space for reflection and escape from the entanglements of his external relationships and responsibilities. This solitary retreat served as a testament to his complex nature, balancing immense professional and personal demands with a deep-seated need for introspection and self-reconciliation.

Vikram Sarabhai's work served as another sanctuary amidst his personal and professional challenges. In the early 1960s, he was instrumental in setting up a satellite telemetry station and a computer centre in Ahmedabad. His involvement extended to various other projects, including joining the board of Gujarat Fertilisers and participating in meetings of the high-powered Electronics Committee in Bombay, established under Homi J Bhabha.

Despite the turmoil in his personal life, Vikram maintained an outward appearance of joviality and light-heartedness. Friends and colleagues recall his ability to make even mundane situations enjoyable, such as bringing jazz records for Navroz Contractor or making light of a wardrobe malfunction on a flight, as recounted by his niece Pallavi Mayor.

His sense of humour and detachment were also evident in more serious situations. Pramod Kale recalls an instance when Vikram humorously cautioned him against discussing the sensitive topic of Kashmir during a dinner at his sister Mridula's house, who was actively campaigning for Sheikh Abdullah's release at the time.

However, the incessant pace and demands of his life began to take a toll on Vikram by the mid-1960s. MS Sastry narrates an incident where Vikram, visibly exhausted, was unable to hold a discussion he had planned with Sastry, indicating a state of physical and mental fatigue. This incident, characterised by his unquenchable thirst and dependency on others, starkly contrasted with his usual energetic persona and hinted at the need for a break that he was unlikely to take.

The period also brought significant challenges to Vikram's family life. His father, Ambalal, suffered a serious illness, his sister Mridula faced legal troubles due to her political activism, and his niece Gita tragically lost her young son. In each of these instances, Vikram's response, whether through support or condolence, demonstrated his deep empathy and connection to his family.

In 1965, the geopolitical landscape of South Asia was also tumultuous. The conflict between India and Pakistan over Kashmir escalated into a full-scale war, drawing international attention and concern. The ceasefire in September and the subsequent Tashkent meeting in early 1966 underscored the region's instability and dependence on foreign aid, as noted by South Asia expert Gunnar Myrdal. Amidst these personal and regional upheavals, Vikram's life was a blend of intense professional dedication, complex personal relationships, and a deep sense of responsibility towards his family and his country.

❑

Life with Bhabha

Vasant Gowarikar's journey from studying chemical engineering in the UK to becoming a pivotal figure in India's space programme is a tale of serendipity and determination. His interest in space was perhaps first kindled when the Nike-Apache rocket illuminated the skies over southern India, an event he read about in local newspapers. This fleeting interest lingered in the back of his mind, surfacing during a casual conversation with Jivraj Mehta, the Indian High Commissioner in the UK and former chief minister of Gujarat, about Gowarikar's potential return to India. Mehta promised to look out for an opportunity for him, though Gowarikar didn't dwell on it, focusing instead on his work on tactical missiles at the Summerfield Research Station.

A pivotal moment arrived in late 1966 when Gowarikar received a letter from Vikram Sarabhai, the architect of the Nike-Apache launch. Sarabhai, then in Geneva, expressed his desire to meet in London. The meeting that followed was transformative. In a hotel, Sarabhai shared his comprehensive vision for India's space programme, including various rockets and stages, and invited Gowarikar to lead the propellant division. Despite Gowarikar's initial hesitation due to his lack of experience in propellants, Sarabhai's confidence and vision were infectious. He famously remarked, "I know nothing about space technology and I am the director!" This left Gowarikar pondering for months until their next meeting.

That second meeting was memorable for Gowarikar. Sarabhai's passionate discourse on his vision, technology, and the concept of 'leapfrogging' in technological advancement left a profound impact. Gowarikar, visibly moved and with 'stars in his eyes', faced a choice presented by Sarabhai: join the Atomic Energy Commission (AEC) in Bombay for a secure path, or embrace the challenge in Trivandrum with the space programme. He chose the latter.

In Trivandrum, Gowarikar encountered a nascent space programme far from the sophisticated facilities Sarabhai had envisioned. Accommodation was scarce, and the early pioneers commuted to Thumba in dilapidated buses, working in a church building so bare it couldn't keep pigeons out. Gowarikar's own office was a repurposed cowshed humorously named 'Gowarikar Nagar', where daily encounters with reptiles and rudimentary safety measures for handling explosives were the norm.

This period was marked by a blend of danger and innovation. Following the successful Nike-Apache launch and a collaboration with the French company Sud Aviation for Centaure sounding rockets, the Indian team trained in France for solid propulsion and hardware fabrication. Back in India, Vikram Sarabhai secured government approval for the Space Science and Technology Centre (SSTC) to develop indigenous sounding rockets, beginning with the Rohini series and followed by Menaka. This naming convention, suggested by Mrinalini Sarabhai and embraced by Vikram for its political resonance, contrasted American rockets named after Greek gods with rockets named after apsaras, figures from Indian mythology.

The early rockets were basic, crafted from aluminium tubes with fins and nozzles, the latter often tied with a rope for retrieval in case of an explosion. Launches were perilous yet exhilarating, with the team seeking shelter behind coconut trees. These rockets were powered by cordite blocks from a Tamil Nadu factory and transported haphazardly across Thumba's rugged terrain. Gowarikar's role was to develop a more sophisticated and suitable rocket fuel, marking the beginning of a significant era in India's space exploration history.

Gowarikar had a big challenge: he didn't know much about polymers, the material he was supposed to work with at the space centre. This wasn't unusual there. For example, Kalam, known as 'busybee', had to figure out how to replace expensive American fibreglass nose-cones without any local examples to follow. Everyone was working on different parts of the technology, starting from scratch.

Vikram Sarabhai, the leader, helped as much as he could. He sent a team to Japan to learn because he believed in learning from Asia rather than always looking to the West. He also got help from his friend S Ramaseshan on the nose-cone issue. Sarabhai was good at managing the team. He would rearrange tasks to reduce pressure and improve work quality, as Kalam said. Sometimes, he brought in experts from abroad to help and challenge the team.

However, Vikram's methods could be tough. He often made team members compete against each other. For instance, Gowarikar and AE Muthunayagam were both working on rocket propellants, and there was a lot of competition between them. They both later claimed that their propellant was used in the first fully Indian rocket. Gowarikar even named his propellant

'Mrinal', which some thought was to impress Sarabhai. This competitive environment was very motivating.

The morale was high, driven by Vikram's encouragement to be innovative. But the programme was always changing. After Vikram died, Satish Dhawan found a growing organisation of over 3,000 people without formal management. There was a committee overseeing operations, but it often argued, although it was united in wanting to show results to Vikram. Gopal Raj admitted it was chaotic but necessary for innovation.

Vikram managed everything well, even from a distance. He visited Thumba every two weeks, checked on everyone's work, and held late-night discussions. His leadership created a trusting and secure environment that motivated everyone. In a country where bureaucracy was heavy, this was very important.

For instance, RG Rastogi remembered how Vikram's influence got him a passport and travel funds quickly for a conference. Once, when there was a dispute with government workers at Thumba, Vikram defended his scientists, saying they should arrest him first. He did more than support his team; he made them feel part of something big and gave them a dream to work towards.

RD John, a civil engineer from the CPWD (Central Public Works Department), initially joined the space programme for what he thought would be a short six-month stint. At first, he questioned the need for rocket firing, but he quickly became a passionate supporter of the programme's ambitious goals, believing that space technology was essential for living. John's commitment led him to a 30-year career in the space programme, eventually becoming the chief engineer of the Department of Space. He developed new specifications for unique requirements, such as computer flooring and special paint for propellant and plane deflection plants.

Many early recruits in the programme went on to hold significant positions. Praful Bhavsar became the programme director for Remote Sensing Applications and chairman of the Remote Sensing Area. EV Chitnis took charge of the Satellite Instructional Television Experiment as project manager and later became the director of the Space Applications Centre. Vasant Gowarikar was appointed as the director of the Vikram Sarabhai Space Centre in Trivandrum, and UR Rao led ISRO from 1984 to 1994.

Gopal Raj noted the remarkable dedication and commitment of the ISRO staff to the goals of the space programme. Despite challenging early conditions, few people left the programme, as they were constantly engaged in overcoming the new challenges posed by Vikram Sarabhai.

In February 1968, Prime Minister Indira Gandhi officially dedicated the Thumba Equatorial Rocket Launch Station (TERLS) to the United Nations in a simple ceremony on the beach. Following this event, Vikram Sarabhai urged his team to begin a full-scale feasibility study on developing a satellite launch vehicle. This idea seemed ambitious since the team had not yet successfully launched a two-stage rocket, but Sarabhai was serious about it. A team began researching suitable models for this project, while Chitnis and Pramod Kale started looking for a launch site on the east coast to benefit from Earth's rotation.

Around the same time, Kalam faced a new challenge from Vikram. In his autobiography, Kalam recalls a meeting with Vikram and Group Captain VS Narayanan from Air Headquarters in Delhi at 3:30 a.m. Vikram presented a plan to develop a rocket-assisted take-off system for military aircraft, particularly useful in the Himalayas. After examining a Russian model, Kalam and Narayanan agreed it was feasible.

Following this meeting, both Kalam and Narayanan joined the newly formed missile panel in the defence ministry. While

Vikram wasn't officially part of this panel, Kalam reveals that he stayed informed about its progress and often received briefings from Kalam after each meeting.

During the exciting times of India's space programme in the mid-1960s, Vikram Sarabhai was also busy with other projects. He established the Nehru Foundation and the Community Science Centre. The idea for the foundation, which focused on development and was a think tank of sorts, came from various inspirations, including Greek architect CA Doxiadis and the intellectual environment of Princeton during World War II. Sarabhai funded the foundation with his own land and the prize money from the SS Bhatnagar Award for Science he received in 1962.

The foundation's first project was setting up facilities where students and adults could learn about science through experiments and various educational materials. In 1965, Vikram met with Axel Horn, a designer of educational programmes, in New York. They planned a programme to give science teachers and students access to resources and scientists not available in public schools. This programme became the basis for the Community Science Centre, built with funds donated by Vikram's mother, Sarla.

While Vikram wasn't directly managing these institutions, his life was increasingly hectic. His wife likened it to walking on a treadmill, always moving but not getting anywhere. And his life became even more complex with some unexpected events.

In January 1966, India faced a series of tragic events. Prime Minister Lal Bahadur Shastri died of a heart attack, and Homi Bhabha, a key figure in India's atomic energy programme, died in an air crash. These events significantly impacted Vikram's life.

This period was tough for India, with wars affecting the economy, rebellions in various regions, and famine in parts of the country. Indira Gandhi, Nehru's daughter, became the new prime minister amid these challenges. She was inexperienced and vulnerable, having had a limited political career and living under the shadow of her father's legacy. Despite her shrewd understanding of politics, gained from years of being close to her father, she faced immense challenges and had many political adversaries.

Indira Gandhi's personal life had also been difficult, marked by loneliness, her mother's poor health, her father's imprisonment, and her own health issues. Her marriage, which had been a source of relief, had deteriorated. On the day she became prime minister, she might have felt overwhelmed, especially with the news of Bhabha's death, which was a significant loss for her and left the atomic energy programme without a leader.

After the passing of Homi Bhabha, Indira Gandhi's advisers initially recommended S Chandrasekhar, a physicist at the University of Chicago and Vikram's friend, to lead the atomic energy programme. However, Chandrasekhar, an American citizen, declined the offer due to potential security issues, a point that seemed to surprise the person who contacted him from the Prime Minister's Office.

Subsequently, Vikram Sarabhai emerged as the leading candidate. While some speculated that Indira Gandhi's choice was politically motivated, especially given her rivalry with Morarji Desai who had previously opposed Vikram's bid for a university position, most experts believed the selection aimed to find someone with enough stature to maintain the programme's domestic and international influence. When Indira asked Vikram to take Bhabha's place, it was a significant moment.

People close to Vikram, like his wife Mrinalini and his mother, were concerned about the impact this role would have on his scientific pursuits, personal life, and the risk of getting entangled in bureaucracy. Vikram himself was well aware of these challenges. It's been suggested that he might have accepted the position partly due to the difficulty of refusing Indira and partly for the influence the position held. However, these reasons don't align well with his character; he had previously turned down public office and was not one to seek the superficial benefits of power.

Vikram's decision seemed more driven by the opportunities the role presented. His family saw it as a natural progression in his career, a chance to fulfil his ambitions for India and expand his impact. Despite understanding the potential personal costs, Vikram accepted the role, seeing it as a unique opportunity to bring his ideas and aspirations to fruition.

Upon accepting the position, Vikram had to make some sacrifices. Due to government regulations against involvement in private enterprises, he resigned from all positions in his family's business. This included leaving Sarabhai Chemicals, a company he had nurtured into a leading pharmaceutical concern. At his farewell, Vikram expressed his emotional attachment to the company, likening it to a garden he had nurtured. His acceptance letter to Indira Gandhi expressed enthusiasm for continuing Bhabha's work and advancing the application of science and technology for the nation, while also clarifying that he would maintain his associations with PRL, the space programme, and MIT.

The Sarabhai family experienced significant upheaval when Vikram Sarabhai decided to take over the leadership of India's atomic energy programme. This sudden shift left Vikram's brother, Gautam, with the added burden of managing the family business. Gita, reflecting on this period, expressed disapproval of how Vikram made this decision without consulting the family, suggesting that a discussion might have eased the transition.

Meanwhile, Vikram didn't stay to address his family's concerns. As officials in Delhi reviewed his business holdings for security clearance, he was travelling for a speaking engagement at Rockefeller University in New York, discussing the role of science and technology in implementing change. After this, he visited Britain, where he surprised some by arriving in a government-loaned car and meeting with Sir John Cockcroft, a prominent figure in the British atomic power programme.

In London, Vikram also met with Raja Ramanna, the head of physics at the Indian Atomic Energy Commission (AEC). Ramanna noted Vikram's readiness to delve into nuclear technology in its entirety.

On 1 June 1966, Vikram officially stepped into his role at the AEC. The media was abuzz with interest, particularly about his stance on nuclear weapons, given his successor Homi Bhabha's prominence in this field.

Bhabha and Vikram, despite being often mentioned together in public memory and even sharing anecdotes attributed to both, were quite different in their personalities and approaches. The space programme, initiated by Vikram, began modestly and unassumingly, situated in a remote area with basic facilities. In contrast, the atomic energy programme under Bhabha was more flamboyant, receiving substantial funding and autonomy, and operating with a high degree of secrecy.

The differences were also evident in the locations and facilities of their respective programmes. The space programme was based in a simple church building in a remote area, while the atomic energy programme had a sprawling, well-designed complex in Bombay. Vikram faced challenges like persuading the Kerala government for infrastructure improvements, whereas Bhabha received active support from the Tamil Nadu government for his projects. These contrasting scenarios highlight the diverse styles and environments that shaped the space and atomic energy programmes in India.

Vikram Sarabhai's decision to lead India's atomic energy programme brought about considerable changes within the

Sarabhai family. This unexpected move placed a significant burden on his brother, Gautam Sarabhai, who suddenly found himself responsible for the family business. Gita Sarabhai, reflecting on this period, expressed her dissatisfaction with Vikram's unilateral decision, suggesting that a family discussion might have made the transition smoother.

As Vikram became occupied with his new responsibilities, he didn't address these family tensions directly. During the period when Delhi officials were conducting security checks on his business interests, Vikram was engaged in international commitments. He delivered a talk at Rockefeller University in New York, focusing on the impact of science and technology on societal change. Subsequently, he visited the UK, where his arrival in a government-loaned car and meeting with Sir John Cockcroft, a key figure in Britain's atomic power programme, came as a surprise to many.

In London, Vikram met Raja Ramanna, the head of physics at the Indian Atomic Energy Commission. Ramanna observed Vikram's thorough preparedness for his role in nuclear technology.

On 1 June 1966, when Vikram Sarabhai officially commenced his role at the AEC, the media was keenly interested in his views, especially regarding nuclear weapons, a domain where his predecessor Homi Bhabha had been a significant figure.

Despite often being conflated in public memory, Homi Bhabha and Vikram Sarabhai had distinctly different personalities and management styles. Vikram's space programme started modestly, with minimal facilities in a remote area. In contrast, Bhabha's atomic energy programme was launched with considerable fanfare, substantial funding, and high levels of autonomy and secrecy.

These differences extended to the physical settings of their respective programmes. The space programme was housed in a simple church building in a remote location, while the atomic energy programme boasted a sprawling, architecturally sophisticated complex in Bombay. Vikram faced challenges like convincing the Kerala government to support infrastructure development, whereas Bhabha enjoyed strong backing from the Tamil Nadu government for his initiatives. These contrasting approaches underscore the distinct paths and environments that shaped India's space and atomic energy programmes under their respective leaders.

The Sarabhai family was deeply impacted when Vikram Sarabhai assumed leadership of India's atomic energy programme. This decision not only affected Vikram's professional life but also had significant implications for his family, particularly his brother Gautam, who suddenly had to take on more responsibilities in managing the family business. Gita Sarabhai, reflecting on this period, expressed her disapproval of Vikram's unilateral decision-making process, suggesting that a more collaborative approach with the family might have eased the transition.

As Vikram embarked on his new role, he didn't stay back to confront the family's concerns. Instead, he was busy with his commitments, including speaking at Rockefeller University in New York on the impact of science and technology on societal change and visiting the UK to meet with key figures in the atomic power programme, including Sir John Cockcroft.

In London, Vikram met with Raja Ramanna, the head of physics at the Indian Atomic Energy Commission (AEC), who noted Vikram's preparedness to fully engage with nuclear technology. On 1 June 1966, Vikram officially started his position at the AEC amidst significant media attention, particularly regarding India's stance on nuclear weapons, following in the footsteps of his predecessor Homi Bhabha.

While both Bhabha and Vikram are often linked in public memory, they had distinct personalities and approaches.

Vikram's space programme was modestly initiated in a remote area with basic facilities, contrasting sharply with Bhabha's atomic energy programme, which was launched with significant funding, autonomy, and secrecy.

The location and infrastructure of their programmes also highlight their different styles. The space programme operated from a simple church building in a remote area, while the atomic energy programme was based in a lush, well-designed complex in Bombay. Vikram had to work hard to persuade the Kerala government for infrastructure development, whereas Bhabha received active support from the Tamil Nadu government for his projects. These contrasting scenarios underscore the diverse paths and environments that shaped India's space and atomic energy programmes under their respective leaders.

Vikram Sarabhai's speech at the Pugwash Conference in Addis Ababa in 1965-66, titled 'Security of Developing Countries', offered a glimpse into his mindset and the perspective he would bring to his new role at India's atomic energy programme. In his address, he highlighted the nuanced complexities of global politics and its impact on developing nations, particularly in the context of nuclear arms proliferation.

Sarabhai began by discussing the world's triangular polarisation in the 1950s, which had led to a kind of mutual neutrality between the East-West blocs and non-aligned countries. This, he argued, inadvertently encouraged developing nations to use force in resolving disputes. He pointed out that nuclear arms, being cheaper than conventional weapons in the long run, made the situation ripe for the spread of nuclear weapons. Furthermore, Sarabhai stressed the detrimental effects of an arms race on the living standards in developing countries and its potential threat to the stability and security of both the big powers and developing nations.

He asserted that the big powers had a responsibility to not only disarm (both nuclear and conventional weapons) but also to establish a system of safeguards and collective security. This system should be able to respond quickly and impartially in cases where one nation's territory is threatened by another. Essentially, Sarabhai was calling on the West to adopt a dual role of moral guide and enforcer.

His views, advocating for disarmament and a balanced approach to global security, were not likely to resonate with his future colleagues at the Atomic Energy Commission (AEC). In particular, Homi N Sethna, a key figure in the AEC and a contender for its leadership following Homi Bhabha's death, was known for his opposition to Sarabhai. Sethna's reputation for efficiency and his ambition to succeed Bhabha led him to an adversarial stance against Sarabhai, often portraying him as an idealistic and impractical leader in the context of nuclear technology and power.

Vikram Sarabhai, with his philosophical leanings and moral reservations about nuclear warfare, was indeed an unconventional choice to head the atomic energy programme. He was firmly against the notion of nuclear warfare, viewing it as a significant threat to human survival. His ideas, while perhaps unpopular, were not formed in naivety; he was a thoughtful and deliberate thinker, deeply aware of the challenges he faced in succeeding Bhabha.

Sarabhai, inspired by Gandhi's principles, believed in the importance of fully understanding and being prepared to endure the consequences of one's actions. Before accepting the AEC position, he acknowledged the difficulties of following in Bhabha's footsteps, recognising it as not just a change in a job but also a transition in thought and approach.

The perception that Vikram Sarabhai's Jain heritage made him less suitable for leading India's atomic energy programme is flawed for a couple of reasons. Firstly, the Sarabhai family, while Jain by tradition, were not dogmatic in their religious practices. Ambalal Sarabhai, Vikram's father, believed in a pragmatic approach to religion and life, even if it occasionally meant compromising strict religious principles, like in the case of non-vegetarianism for medicinal purposes. Vikram similarly displayed a pragmatic approach in his beliefs and actions.

Moreover, the idea that Jainism's principle of non-violence equates to weakness or passivity is a misinterpretation. Lawrence Babb, in clarifying this misconception, explains that Jainism actually incorporates martial values in a transformed way. The Jina, or spiritual conqueror in Jainism, is seen as a figure who could have been a worldly king and conqueror but chose to become a spiritual leader instead. The religion emphasises the idea of inner struggle and conquest, turning the battlefield from an external to an internal one. This philosophy of transmuted martial valour is integral to Jain thought.

Vikram's mindset in accepting the AEC leadership role can be understood through this lens. He was fully aware of the challenges and potential setbacks but was likely driven by a moral imperative, similar to Gandhi's approach of moral dominance in mediation.

When Vikram took charge, he brought a new perspective to the atomic energy discourse. Unlike Bhabha's more ambitious and less nuanced approach, Vikram's understanding of atomic energy for development or defence was more carefully calibrated. He questioned the practical benefits of nuclear capability for India rather than focusing solely on the prestige it might bring. During a crucial press conference in June 1966, Vikram emphasised that real security isn't achieved by merely possessing a nuclear bomb. He argued that security involves a comprehensive defence system and a balance between defence spending and economic development.

Vikram's stance marked a departure from the prevailing enthusiasm for nuclear demonstration. However, contrary to what some believed, he didn't outright reject atomic weapons as a means of national security. His opposition was more towards adopting an aggressive military stance without the necessary infrastructure and means to support it. He advocated for a balanced and pragmatic approach to national security and resource utilisation.

Vikram Sarabhai's perspective on India's nuclear programme was grounded in a holistic understanding of the nation's priorities and needs. He emphasised the importance of building a robust internal infrastructure, including a strong metallurgical and electronics base, as prerequisites to developing more advanced technologies like missile systems. Sarabhai believed in the step-by-step development of the country's grassroots economy, which he saw as fundamental to any further technological advancements.

In his private notes from around 1966, Vikram expressed concern over broader social issues, such as the cynicism of the older generation and the disconnection between their actions and their preaching. This reflection on societal values and the younger generation's protests worldwide suggests that his approach was deeply rooted in a desire for social progress and ethical governance.

At the June press conference, Sarabhai chose to focus on the economic implications of nuclear armament—the classic 'guns versus butter' dilemma. This perspective wasn't new; commentators like Romesh Thapar had previously expressed similar views, noting that possessing a nuclear bomb doesn't elevate a nation's status if it lacks other fundamental capabilities. While Sarabhai's stance might have seemed unexpected from someone in his position at the AEC, it reflected his belief in prioritising national development over nuclear armament.

Vikram's approach marked a shift in the atomic energy programme's focus from Bhabha's more personalised leadership to a more regulatory and development-oriented phase. He actively engaged with the programme's technical aspects and facilitated international exposure for AEC scientists to the latest trends in reactor technology and nuclear applications. This included study tours to the US, USSR and France, demonstrating his commitment to redirecting the programme towards peaceful energy production.

The renaming of the atomic energy establishment at Trombay to the Bhabha Atomic Research Centre (BARC) in 1967 exemplifies Vikram's respect for Bhabha's vision and his efforts to continue international cooperation for peaceful atomic uses. By praising Bhabha's commitment to peaceful applications, Vikram reiterated India's stance on using nuclear technology for constructive purposes.

Sarabhai's responses at the press conference also signified a shift in the nuclear weapons debate from a purely scientific or technological perspective to a broader political one. He asserted that the decision to develop nuclear weapons was not just technological but also political, requiring careful consideration of the nation's overall interests and resources.

During this period, Prime Minister Indira Gandhi faced numerous challenges, including severe famine and political pressures. Sarabhai, seen as a trusted adviser, played a crucial role in advising and shaping the government's approach to these complex issues, demonstrating the intersection of science, technology and politics in national decision-making.

Vikram Sarabhai's relationship with Prime Minister Indira Gandhi was characterised by a blend of professional respect and personal friendliness. Both being of a similar age and having married in the same year, they shared a common understanding of the need to balance traditional heritage with the technological revolution. Vikram and his wife Mrinalini embodied the blend of cultural depth and scientific progress that Indira valued.

Indira's informal interactions with Vikram, like the playful note about the curtains at a science meeting, indicated a level of comfort and trust in their relationship. Vikram, known for his discipline and respect for hierarchy, maintained a proper professional demeanour with the prime minister. However, there were instances, such as the exchange of a single red rose, that suggested a light-hearted and slightly flirtatious aspect to their interactions.

As Vikram took charge of the AEC, his stance on nuclear weapons, emphasising India's internal development and economic priorities, gained support from various quarters. KC Pant, a key political figure, echoed Vikram's views, shifting from a previously robust stance on nuclear policy to one advocating against deciding on nuclear weapons at that time. This shift paralleled the arguments made by India's envoy to the UN advocating for non-proliferation and the rights of non-nuclear states.

Major General Som Dutt's analysis further reinforced Vikram's position. Dutt argued that the costs of nuclear weaponisation outweighed the benefits for India, considering factors like security threats, war effectiveness, and international relations. This comprehensive assessment aligned with Vikram's approach, which looked outward and considered the broader implications of nuclear weaponisation, in contrast to the more inward-looking perspective of Homi Bhabha.

By late 1966, the momentum for acquiring nuclear weapons in India had diminished. India's agreement with Canada for a second power reactor, which included stringent safeguards and an emphasis on using Indian components, reflected the shift from Bhabha's era to Vikram's more cautious approach. The announcement of new nuclear facilities in India occurred against the backdrop of China's nuclear tests, which elicited little reaction in India, indicating a change in the country's nuclear discourse.

Internationally, the focus was shifting towards non-proliferation with the Nuclear Non-Proliferation Treaty (NPT), though India criticised this approach as it emphasised stopping the spread of nuclear weapons without addressing disarmament. The US's offer to provide peaceful nuclear explosives was seen by India as patronising, reinforcing its role as a central voice in the global debate on nuclear policy. This scenario underscored India's engagement with philosophical questions and its significant role in shaping the international discourse on nuclear issues.

The debate within India shifted from whether to produce nuclear weapons to whether the country should sign a treaty relinquishing the right to do so. A significant group of influential Indians, representing both pro- and anti-nuclear weapon perspectives, urged the government not to sign the treaty being formulated by the superpowers. The Lok Sabha, too, expressed hope for improvements in the treaty.

Vikram Sarabhai, deeply engaged in these discussions, faced the challenge of maintaining confidentiality due to the secretive nature of atomic energy matters. His views on nuclear weapons can be inferred from his notes, observations of those around him, and his actions. A note from February 1966 suggests he was contemplating non-proliferation and the need for restraint among both nuclear and non-nuclear states even before becoming chairman of the AEC.

As chairman in 1967, Sarabhai collaborated with LK Jha, principal secretary to Prime Minister Indira Gandhi, to develop an alternative to the discriminatory non-proliferation treaty. They focused on nuclear blackmail as a significant threat to non-nuclear states. Their proposed solution was a multilateral guarantee from superpowers to protect non-nuclear states from nuclear threats, aiming to discourage them from pursuing nuclear capabilities.

Sarabhai and Jha's approach received serious consideration from the Indian Government, a testament to Sarabhai's influence. They embarked on an international campaign, presenting their proposal to various state capitals, including Moscow, Washington, London and Paris. However, their efforts met with lukewarm responses due to various geopolitical factors.

In a meeting with US Defence Secretary Robert McNamara, Sarabhai emphasised that India's reluctance to accept the NPT did not imply a hidden desire to build nuclear weapons. His stance was seen as a continuation of Nehru's strategy of ambiguity, leaving open the possibility of pursuing peaceful nuclear explosions. Sarabhai's discussions revealed his deep commitment to a nuclear-free world, emphasising the moral imperative and the dangers of the nuclear path.

Despite the lack of guarantees, India decided not to sign the NPT in May 1967 while also committing not to produce nuclear weapons, a stance reaffirmed by Defence Minister Swaran Singh.

Amidst these professional challenges, Sarabhai adapted to a significant change in his personal life. His role as chairman of the AEC required him to move to Bombay, where he lived alone in Kashmir House, a family-owned property, while his wife Mrinalini remained in Ahmedabad due to her commitments with her dance school.

Vikram Sarabhai's life during his tenure at the Atomic Energy Commission (AEC) was a blend of professional dedication and personal adjustments. Despite his significant public role, he maintained warm relationships with his family, particularly with his sister Gita, who lived close to him. His involvement in family financial matters, like considering 'estate duty' and 'Ambalal's estate', suggests that he wasn't entirely detached from the family's financial affairs, though he didn't interfere in the business after resigning from Sarabhai Chemicals.

His personal life was marked by a degree of loneliness, with Kamla engaged with the Indian Institute of Management (IIM) and his son, Kartikeya, studying abroad. While Kartikeya chose not to pursue a career in science, Vikram supported his decision, emphasising the importance of completing his education. Meanwhile, his relationship with his daughter Mallika improved, evolving into a close bond marked by deep conversations and shared interests.

Professionally, Vikram's focus shifted from national to international platforms. In 1968, he played a prominent role as the Scientific Chairman at the United Nations Conference on the Exploration and Peaceful Uses of Outer Space. His speech there echoed his consistent theme of global interdependence and the need for sharing knowledge and technology. He emphasised that restricting technology transfer, especially in peaceful space applications, could harm global security by hindering the progress of nations.

Vikram's scientific work also continued, particularly in the field of cosmic rays. He engaged in building physical models to account for observed anisotropies in cosmic rays, a challenging task involving the analysis of precise and comprehensive observational data. This work contributed to the understanding of space phenomena and confirmed aspects of Parker's model, including the detection of rotating shocks that Vikram had predicted.

Throughout these years, Vikram's commitment to a nuclear-free world and his belief in the moral imperative of peaceful uses of technology remained central to his actions and advocacy, both nationally and internationally. His approach to nuclear policy and space technology reflected a blend of scientific rigour, ethical considerations, and a deep understanding of India's socio-economic context.

Vikram Sarabhai's visits to Thumba, the site of the Space Science and Technology Centre (SSTC), were marked by intense activity and productivity. Abdul Kalam, who later became a prominent figure in India's space programme, detailed Sarabhai's typical schedule during these fortnightly visits, showcasing his hands-on approach and commitment to various aspects of the space programme.

An average day for Sarabhai in Thumba would begin with the observation of a Rohini-100 motor flight test. Despite occasional failures, such as the one mentioned by Kalam, Sarabhai's response was always encouraging, urging the project leader to persevere. His day would include a diverse range of activities, from discussing building plans for the SSTC with John to finalising control flight plans for the RH-125 test, which were crucial for the inauguration of the Satish Dhawan Space Centre, SHAR (Sriharikota Range).

Sarabhai's involvement extended to witnessing successful rocket flights and engaging in extensive review sessions on critical projects like the preliminary design study of the Satellite Launch Vehicle-3 (SLV3). His attention to detail was evident in his visits to the gyro laboratory, where he examined precision components, an essential aspect of space technology.

These packed schedules, often resulting in Sarabhai leaving with a hefty load of reports, highlighted his role as a dynamic leader who was deeply involved in the minutiae of India's space programme. Abdul Kalam's analogy of Sarabhai as a 'resourceful farmer harvesting loads of grain from his selective seedings' aptly captures the essence of Sarabhai's approach: nurturing, hands-on, and focused on reaping the benefits of well-planned and executed projects. Sarabhai's leadership style was instrumental in laying the foundation for India's future successes in space exploration and technology.

❑

Difficult Times

Vikram Sarabhai's commitment to indigenisation and self-reliance in technology was a cornerstone of his vision for India's development. This principle was put to the test when the Indian Government decided to contract Canadians to build an Earth station for a satellite loaned by the Americans. Sarabhai, distressed by this decision, passionately argued against relying on outsiders for such critical infrastructure. His question to IK Gujral, then Minister of State for Communications, "Where will the Indians experiment if not in India?" and his rhetorical query, "Will the Canadians ask us to build it for them?" reflected his deep belief in nurturing Indian expertise and capability.

PN Haksar, the principal secretary to the prime minister at the time, also witnessed Sarabhai's agitation over this issue. It was uncharacteristic for Sarabhai, known for his composure, to display such emotion. His frustration was rooted in the challenges of navigating the bureaucratic system of the Indian Government, which he felt was impeding the realisation of his vision for the country.

Sarabhai proposed a collaborative approach to Haksar, where he would share his frustrations, and Haksar, with his extensive experience, would help find solutions. This partnership was indicative of Sarabhai's determination to overcome bureaucratic hurdles.

Sarabhai's advocacy for indigenisation wasn't just a philosophical stance; it was backed by practical actions and proposals. As head of the electronics committee, he recommended guidelines for research and development and operational efficiency. His initiatives led to the establishment of the Electronics Prototype Engineering Laboratory at BARC and the creation of a separate ministerial wing for electronics.

While Sarabhai supported exposure to advanced Western technology, believing that India's first satellite should be built and launched abroad for the sake of timely development and learning, he was staunchly against importing outdated technologies. He envisioned India leapfrogging developmental stages by adopting current technologies as economically as possible.

Ultimately, Sarabhai's persistence paid off. With the support of influential figures like Haksar and Gujral, and eventually the prime minister herself, the government relented, allowing him to proceed with building the Earth station in India. This decision was a significant win for Sarabhai's vision of fostering Indian technological expertise and self-reliance.

Vikram Sarabhai was a staunch advocate for India's technological autonomy and this philosophy was put to the test when the government planned to outsource the construction of an Earth station to Canadian contractors. This was for a satellite that the Americans had offered to loan. Sarabhai, deeply troubled by this decision, made a strong case for developing such critical infrastructure indigenously. He challenged IK Gujral, the then Minister of State for Communications, with pointed questions about the opportunities for Indian innovation and the absurdity of relying on foreign nations for domestic technological needs.

PN Haksar, serving as the principal secretary to the prime minister then, witnessed Sarabhai's rare display of agitation, signalling his frustration with the bureaucratic barriers hindering his vision for India. Sarabhai proposed a solution: he would express his concerns to Haksar, who would then use his experience to navigate these obstacles, reflecting a strategic partnership to tackle bureaucratic challenges.

Sarabhai's commitment to domestic technological development wasn't mere rhetoric. He actively sought practical measures, heading the electronics committee and suggesting strategies for research and development. His efforts led to the creation of the Electronics Prototype Engineering Laboratory at BARC and a dedicated ministerial wing for electronics. Sarabhai believed in assimilating cutting-edge Western technology to expedite India's developmental journey, yet he vehemently opposed the import of outdated foreign technologies.

Persistence and strategic alliances with key governmental figures like Haksar and Gujral, and support from the prime minister, eventually led the government to authorise the construction of the Earth station within India. This triumph was a significant stride towards realising Sarabhai's dream of an India self-reliant in technology and innovation.

Vikram Sarabhai's drive to revolutionise communication technology in India, particularly through television, was rooted in his vision to uplift the rural masses despite not having extensive personal experience with village life. His life was predominantly urban, and there are no notable mentions of him spending significant time in rural or underdeveloped areas. However, his keen interest in impacting these communities was evident in his initiatives.

Sarabhai's understanding of television as a medium was not necessarily as a regular viewer, as even he, despite his extensive travels, may not have watched much television. The concept of television was relatively new in India during his time, with radio just becoming a mass medium.

Despite this, Sarabhai had a clear vision for using television as a tool for educational and developmental communication. He was aware of potential ground-level challenges such as audience receptivity and maintenance issues. His determination to address these problems is exemplified by his remark about deploying a helicopter for set maintenance if necessary, quoted by his colleague BS Bhatia.

Sarabhai's foresight in communication technology continues to influence discussions on ideal formats for Indian television. However, the eventual evolution of television in India—first as a government propaganda tool and later dominated by entertainment—might suggest that Sarabhai underestimated the complexities of human nature and media consumption.

Yet, Sarabhai's ideas about advanced technology enabling freedom and decentralisation, akin to his analogy of a computer network, were quite prophetic. His vision of delivering information directly to individuals, like farmers, to foster development at various levels rather than creating large urban conglomerates, somewhat anticipated the impact of the internet.

Amidst his professional endeavours, Sarabhai's personal life was busy and he travelled extensively for meetings and collaborations. He managed a hectic schedule with the help of his devoted personal secretaries, NVG Warrier and KR Ramnath, who catered to his needs and eccentricities. His lifestyle was marked by meticulous planning and attention to personal hygiene, and his secretaries were attentive to his preferences and health.

TN Seshan, a Tamil IAS (Indian Administrative Service) officer overseeing the AEC secretariat, became another significant figure in Sarabhai's life. Despite the typical bureaucratic distance from the Department of Atomic Energy, Seshan's interest in nuclear energy economics and his assertive personality led to a strong working relationship with Sarabhai. This dynamic between a scientist and a bureaucrat illustrated the multifaceted nature of Sarabhai's leadership and his ability to collaborate across different professional realms.

Vikram Sarabhai, amidst the challenging environment at the Department of Atomic Energy (DAE), relied on a support system of trusted individuals to navigate the complexities and implement his ambitious plans. His ten-year profile for the decade of 1970-80 included advanced projects like building 500MW enriched uranium reactors and accelerating the fast breeder reactor programme. These plans indicated his daring vision, though they weren't universally accepted within the department.

Sarabhai encountered resistance and scepticism from several colleagues at the DAE. For example, MR Srinivasan, a senior engineer, and others like Homi Sethna and R Ramanna were wary of Sarabhai's enthusiasm for certain technologies. This contrasted with the warm reception Sarabhai's ideas usually received in the space programme. His attempts to restructure the AEC and initiatives at the Electronics Corporation of India Limited (ECIL) also met with resistance.

Despite the technological challenges and reservations, Sarabhai's initiatives in other areas, such as management studies and training at the DAE, were more successful. However, the debate over India's nuclear weapons programme posed a significant challenge. There was a divergence of opinion within the Trombay scientific community regarding the development of nuclear weapons, with many viewing it as a measure of technological mastery and national security.

While there was some progress in research on nuclear weapons before Sarabhai's tenure, it was limited due to insufficient know-how and lack of fissile material. Despite claims that Sarabhai had halted the SNEPP (Study of Nuclear Explosions for Peaceful Purposes) programme, work on nuclear weapons design reportedly continued, possibly without his intervention. This situation reflected the complexity of navigating leadership in a field with diverse and strong opinions.

Sarabhai's leadership style at the DAE remained consistent, marked by his usual charm and approachability, despite the resistance he faced. He managed to create a positive environment, even as he dealt with challenging dynamics, particularly with Homi Sethna, who was openly antagonistic towards him. Sarabhai's approach to conflict was to defuse tensions rather than confront them directly, often choosing to discuss issues privately or counter objections through memoranda.

Despite the struggles and the intricate politics of the DAE, Sarabhai continued to enjoy simple pleasures like his boat rides from the Gateway of India to Trombay. He managed multiple meetings simultaneously, displaying a calm and collected demeanour even amid heated discussions. His endearing presence and ability to connect with colleagues at all levels distinguished his leadership at the AEC, even as he navigated through the complex web of opinions and resistance within the department.

Vikram Sarabhai's response to the hostility he faced at the Department of Atomic Energy (DAE), particularly from Homi Sethna, has been subject to two contrasting interpretations. Some viewed his non-confrontational approach as a lack of robustness in dealing with aggression. This view is supported by observations from acquaintances like Kamal Mangaldas and Prakash Tandon, who saw Sarabhai as somewhat naïve or incapable of saying 'no'. UR Rao's anecdote about Sarabhai's hypothetical reaction to a personal affront further illustrates this perception of him as non-confrontational.

However, an alternative interpretation suggests that Sarabhai's behaviour was not due to timidity but rather a conscious choice of restraint. His colleagues often noted him controlling his emotions, implying he was capable of strong feelings but chose to manage them deliberately. UR Rao recounts Sarabhai's insistence on collaboration between scientists and engineers, and TN Seshan believed that Sarabhai would have preferred to make an ally out of Sethna rather than confront him. Mallika Sarabhai, his daughter, reflected that her father believed in the right to disagree and in educating others on different perspectives rather than resorting to aggression.

Sarabhai often met opposition with patience and explanation, even in situations where others expected a more forceful response. His approach was more in line with a scientist's method of resolving issues through experimentation and discussion, rather than confrontation.

In his personal life, Sarabhai sought resolutions that included all parties in harmony, a reflection of his tendency to reconcile opposing forces. This tendency extended to his professional life, where he attempted to bring together divergent viewpoints within the DAE.

From 1968 onwards, Sarabhai's actions suggested a nuanced stance on India's nuclear policy. He sent a delegation led by PK Iyengar to the Soviet Union, leading to the inception of the 'Plutonium Reactor for Neutron Investigation in Multiplying Assemblies (Purnima)', which aligned with India's long-term plans involving fast breeder reactors. This move was seen by some, like Iyengar, as an indication of Sarabhai's support for acquiring the necessary physics for nuclear capabilities.

Sarabhai's meeting with K Subrahmanyam, a young deputy secretary in the defence ministry, further complicates the narrative. Subrahmanyam, who had a pro-nuclear stance, likely had a detailed and extended discussion with Sarabhai, indicating that Sarabhai's views on India's nuclear policy were more complex than a simple pro- or anti-nuclear position. This meeting underscores the multifaceted and strategic nature of Sarabhai's approach to India's nuclear capabilities and policy.

Vikram Sarabhai's approach to India's nuclear policy and technological development was characterised by a nuanced understanding and a balance between humanitarian concerns and scientific progress. This complexity is evident in his interactions with KSubrahmanyam, a defence policy expert, and others within the scientific community.

Sarabhai's conversations with Subrahmanyam revealed an open-minded yet cautious stance on nuclear weapons. While not outright opposing the development of nuclear capabilities for future generations, Sarabhai maintained that he was not in favour of pursuing nuclear armament in the present context. This position reflects a recognition of the need to keep technological options open for future needs without committing to a specific path immediately.

Homi Sethna, another key figure in India's nuclear programme, believed that Sarabhai became more inclined towards nuclear armament after his diplomatic efforts for an alternative approach to non-proliferation did not yield the desired results. This perspective, however, is contrasted with Kartikeya Sarabhai's view that his father never fully decided on the nuclear weapons issue.

Sarabhai's approach can be understood as a blend of humanitarianism and scientific pragmatism. He believed in exploring all technological possibilities without necessarily committing to their immediate application, particularly in the context of nuclear weapons. This stance is reminiscent of the philosophical and scientific principles he admired, such as Gandhi's belief in inherent 'good' in people and the dual nature of light as both particles and waves, indicating an acceptance of complexity and ambivalence.

In the realm of energy, Sarabhai was actively involved in advancing India's nuclear power projects, particularly the fast breeder reactor programme, which was crucial for India's energy security given its limited uranium resources. His efforts in this area included seeking international collaboration and establishing research centres.

Sarabhai's commitment to the space programme was equally significant. Under his leadership, the Indian Space Research Organisation (ISRO) was established, marking a major milestone in India's space exploration journey. His personal involvement in the development of the satellite launching station at Sriharikota and his choice to stay in a modest guest house in Kovalam during visits to the space centre illustrated his hands-on approach and dedication to the project.

Throughout his career, Sarabhai navigated complex scientific, bureaucratic and political landscapes, striking a balance between advancing technological capabilities and adhering to a humanitarian vision. His legacy in shaping India's scientific and technological policies continues to influence the country's progress in these fields.

During the late 1960s and early 1970s, Vikram Sarabhai's leadership and innovative approach were manifest in various groundbreaking projects and initiatives, even as he navigated the complex political and scientific landscape of India's nuclear policy.

At Thumba, the development of the Satellite Launch Vehicle (SLV) was progressing under Sarabhai's guidance. He divided the project into four segments, each led by different scientists including AE Muthunayagam, MR Kurup, and APJ Abdul Kalam. This decentralised leadership style, however, led some to believe that Sarabhai struggled to relinquish control.

In a chance meeting with Kirit Parikh, a young professor from the Indian Statistical Institute, Sarabhai demonstrated his openness to new ideas. This encounter led to the establishment of the Programme Analysis Group (PAG) under Parikh's leadership, tasked with analysing DAE activities from an economic and marketing perspective.

Despite these advancements, Sarabhai faced challenges within the political context. The Congress Party split, and Prime Minister Indira Gandhi's populist measures created an atmosphere of uncertainty. Meanwhile, Ahmedabad, Sarabhai's hometown, experienced communal violence, which deeply disturbed him.

Internationally, the debate over peaceful nuclear explosions (PNEs) was intensifying. Sarabhai was set to preside over the 1970 Vienna Conference of the International Atomic Energy Agency (IAEA), a significant event following the contentious negotiations over the Nuclear Non-Proliferation Treaty (NPT). At this conference, R Chidambaram made a presentation on peaceful nuclear explosion applications, indicating ongoing research in this area within India.

Despite his humanitarian outlook, Sarabhai's actions suggested a pragmatic approach to nuclear technology. He was aware of the work on explosives design being conducted by R Chidambaram and others, and his interactions implied tacit support for acquiring such technological capabilities.

However, the growing hawkish sentiment in India, particularly after China's successful long-range rocket launch, posed a challenge to Sarabhai's vision. A public opinion study revealed a significant shift in attitudes towards India developing nuclear capabilities, though support waned when juxtaposed with the cost of cutting development expenditure.

Amidst these developments, Sarabhai continued to balance his roles, ensuring the successful inauguration of India's first nuclear power station in Tarapur and promoting peaceful uses of nuclear technology. His legacy remains a testament to his multifaceted approach, combining scientific rigour with a commitment to humanitarian principles.

The Sarabhai Profile, detailing India's plan for atomic energy and space for the decade of 1970-1980, was initially met with national approval. However, it was only officially adopted by the government in 1971, following Indira Gandhi's significant electoral victory.

Amidst his numerous official responsibilities, Vikram Sarabhai continued to engage in various activities. He met Neil Armstrong, the first man on the moon, in Bombay and even viewed a moon rock. Additionally, he supported the cause of population control, a topic he discussed with his sister-in-law, Dr Lakshmi Sehgal. Despite some criticism, particularly regarding his advocacy of male sterilisation, Sarabhai remained committed to addressing India's population growth.

Sarabhai also found time for family. He introduced his daughter Mallika to golf in Gulmarg and cared for his son and daughter-in-law in the US when they fell ill. He even attended a ballet in Venice with Mallika, displaying his ability to balance family life with his professional commitments.

However, this constant activity took a toll on Sarabhai. To manage his busy lifestyle, he occasionally took two-hour sleep breaks, during which his colleagues made sure not to disturb him. In 1970, the birth of his grandson brought immense joy to Sarabhai, and he enjoyed spending time with his family at his new residence, which featured a roof garden facilitated by IG Patel, who cleverly navigated the financial approval process.

Yet, as 1970 ended and Indira Gandhi called for new elections, political changes were on the horizon. The elections, fought on the 'Garibi Hatao' (Remove Poverty) slogan, saw Indira Gandhi securing a commanding victory, bringing her back to power with a significant majority. This period also highlighted the strong professional relationship between Sarabhai and Indira Gandhi, particularly their shared perspectives on issues like nuclear weapons and national security. Their views were aligned in prioritising conventional military preparedness over nuclear armament, recognising the potential economic burden and threat to internal security posed by nuclear weapons.

During the late 1960s, the political and scientific landscape in India was undergoing significant changes, and Vikram Sarabhai found himself at the centre of these developments. His involvement in various projects, including discussions on RATO systems for military aircraft with APJ Abdul Kalam and others, showcased his multifaceted role in India's technological advancement.

Sarabhai's engagement with Neil Armstrong and his support for population control initiatives further illustrated his wide range of interests. However, his support for population control, particularly male sterilisation, was met with some criticism, though Sarabhai remained convinced of its necessity for India.

Politically, Indira Gandhi was solidifying her position, winning against the old guard within the Congress Party. However, this consolidation of power led to a transformation in her character, making her increasingly suspicious and intolerant of others, as observed by PC Alexander and Raj Thapar.

A potential rift between Sarabhai and Indira Gandhi began to emerge in this period. Concerns from senior atomic energy scientists about any potential concessions made by Sarabhai and LK Jha in their diplomatic efforts might have influenced Indira Gandhi. These scientists, viewing themselves as guardians of India's security, were apprehensive about forfeiting nuclear options. Indira Gandhi's growing inclination to play different parties against each other could have exacerbated this situation.

The debate was not just about developing a nuclear weapons programme, where Sarabhai's stance was ambiguous, but also about the need for a demonstration of India's nuclear capabilities. Sarabhai was opposed to such a demonstration, considering it a 'paper tiger'. However, the demand for a demonstration was resurfacing, and by this time, India had both the knowledge and the necessary materials more readily available.

Indira Gandhi's request for feasibility studies on a long-range ballistic missile and a nuclear-propelled submarine indicated her interest in military expansion. Notably, around mid-1970, she reportedly asked Sarabhai to prepare for a nuclear explosion. Sarabhai's subsequent assertion about India's capability for underground nuclear explosions further supports this.

However, this period was marked by considerable stress for Sarabhai, especially regarding the prime minister's advisers and the potential impact on his space programme. Despite reduced funding for the space programme, Sarabhai maintained his characteristic enthusiasm.

In May 1971, Sarabhai took a rare family vacation in Manali, where he seemingly unwound, engaging in leisure activities and spending time with his family. Despite the presence of security, indicative of his prominent position, Sarabhai and his family managed to enjoy a brief respite from the intensifying pressures and complexities of his professional life.

❑

Last Breath

In 1971, as Vikram Sarabhai grappled with the escalating pressures of his professional life, internal conflicts and external political changes intensified. The cost-benefit analysis on peaceful nuclear explosives he commissioned showed economic viability, increasing pressure on him. Despite this, Sarabhai maintained a composed exterior, although privately, he was deeply troubled.

His daughter Mallika observed that Sarabhai was influenced by a Gandhian ethos of self-sufficiency, which perhaps contributed to his internal struggle. A telling incident occurred when Sarabhai unexpectedly woke up one night, distressed about his work, revealing the immense stress he was under.

Publicly, Sarabhai continued to advocate for nuclear explosive engineering at international forums like the Fourth International Conference on Peaceful Uses of Atomic Energy in Geneva. However, his private conversations indicated a more complex stance. He informed K Subrahmanyam and Sisir Gupta about an invitation from France to observe a nuclear test, suggesting his involvement with the pro-nuclear demonstration lobby.

Amidst these developments, India's political landscape was also shifting. Indira Gandhi's government was dealing with the refugee crisis from East Pakistan and the impending conflict with Pakistan. Sarabhai, undeterred by the war tensions, focused on identifying sites for agro-industrial complexes.

Within the Atomic Energy Commission (AEC), tensions were mounting. Homi Sethna was becoming restless for a leadership change, and there were rumours that Indira Gandhi might separate the space programme from the AEC, leaving Sarabhai to choose between the two. Despite these pressures, Sarabhai did not openly express any distress.

When the Indo-Pak War broke out in December 1971, Sarabhai remained dedicated to his work, even suggesting the use of sounding rockets from the space programme as makeshift missiles. The war ended with Pakistan's surrender, but the strain on Sarabhai was evident.

In his personal interactions, Sarabhai continued to show warmth and attentiveness, but hints of his inner turmoil surfaced. A chance encounter with a snake during a run in Kovalam led him to believe that his problems were resolving, reflecting a rare superstitious side.

Towards the end of 1971, Sarabhai's interactions with his family in Ahmedabad were affectionate, yet he expressed a longing for a simpler life, away from the pressures of his high-profile roles. His desire to retire and teach science to children at the Community Science Centre was a poignant indication of his yearning for peace amidst the tumultuous demands of his professional life.

Vikram Sarabhai's final days in December 1971 were a mix of professional commitments and personal moments. Despite exhaustion, he returned to Bombay from Ahmedabad, ready for a busy schedule, including a routine trip to Thumba. Amidst this, he found time to support his daughter Mallika, who faced criticism for her decision to act in a film, a choice that echoed the challenges his wife Mrinalini had faced years earlier in her dance career.

Sarabhai's travel plans were often hectic, and a last-minute meeting on the Satellite Instructional Television Experiment (SITE) required him to fly to Delhi with Raja Ramanna. During the flight, he spoke about his blood pressure problem and his interest in yoga, a surprising revelation given his connection to pharmaceuticals.

After a day in Delhi, Sarabhai was set to leave for Thumba the next morning. Mallika, hoping for a family New Year celebration, pleaded with him not to go, but he promised to join them in Ahmedabad in a few days. They parted ways early the next morning, each heading to their respective commitments.

Sarabhai's time in Thumba on 28 and 29 December was filled with meetings and discussions. He interacted with various colleagues, including RD John, HGS Murthy, and members of the chemicals group. Despite the challenges, he remained optimistic, focusing on building the group. A meeting with other ISRO members followed, and the evening was spent in lively conversation.

That night, Gowarikar noticed Sarabhai lying on the floor in an unusual posture, which he later mentioned to his wife. After the meetings, Sarabhai finalised plans for the next day, including a swim with Gowarikar and a meeting with Kalam at the airport.

However, the morning of 30 December brought a sombre turn. Sarabhai did not respond to the calls of the room staff at the Kovalam guest house. Concerned, they eventually entered his room to find him lying motionless, a book on his chest. The doctor who arrived declared that Sarabhai had likely passed away a couple of hours earlier. His peaceful appearance led Mrs Shandamma to remark that he seemed to be merely sleeping.

Vikram Sarabhai's unexpected passing marked the end of an era in Indian science and technology. His contributions to the fields of space and nuclear science and his visionary leadership left an indelible mark on India's scientific landscape.

Vikram Sarabhai's untimely death on 30 December1971, sent shockwaves across India, deeply affecting those who knew him and the many whose lives he had touched. News of his passing brought a wave of grief and disbelief in various circles.

At Trivandrum airport, a sombre mood prevailed, with Abdul Kalam learning of Sarabhai's death upon his arrival. In Bangalore, Air Marshal Mehra and Prakash Tandon, who were expecting to meet Sarabhai, received the sad news at the airport. Anil Majumdar in Baroda got the news from a journalist, leading to a sombre atmosphere at Sarabhai Chemicals. In Ahmedabad, Leena was shocked when she received a call from Sarla informing her of Vikram's demise.

At Bombay airport, Mrinalini and Mallika Sarabhai, along with a crowd of notable figures and admirers, awaited the arrival of Vikram's body. The next day, major newspapers, including the Times of India, paid tribute to the space research pioneer.

In Ahmedabad, a procession carried Vikram's body to the Sarabhai family's farm at Hansol village for the funeral. Despite plans for a private event, the gates were opened to the public due to Vikram's status as a public figure, drawing a large and diverse crowd. The ceremony was marked by profound grief, with many attendees visibly moved.

Mallika Sarabhai performed the rare and historic act of lighting her father's pyre, a task traditionally reserved for male family members. This decision was practical due to Kartikeya's absence, but it also had significant cultural implications.

Following the funeral, Vikram Sarabhai's ashes were scattered in the Indian Ocean near Thumba. That year, the

Sabarmati River flooded, washing away the remains of the pyre at Hansol.

In recognition of his contributions to space science, the International Astronomical Union named a moon crater after Dr Vikram Sarabhai in 1974, calling it the Sarabhai Crater. This honour is a testament to the lasting impact of his work and the deep respect he garnered in the global scientific community.

*****

Vikram Sarabhai, a visionary in the field of space research and atomic energy, left an indelible mark on India's scientific landscape. His untimely demise on 30 December 1971, brought an end to a dynamic and transformative career, but his legacy continues to inspire.

Sarabhai's contributions to India's space programme were monumental. As the founder of the Indian Space Research Organisation (ISRO), he laid the foundation for India's achievements in space exploration. His vision of using space technology for national development, particularly in communication, meteorology and education, has been realised over the years, with ISRO becoming a significant player in global space research.

In the field of atomic energy, Sarabhai's tenure as the chairman of the Atomic Energy Commission was marked by a nuanced approach. He balanced the pursuit of nuclear technology for peaceful purposes with a humanitarian perspective, advocating against nuclear armament while recognising the importance of maintaining technological prowess.

Sarabhai's influence extended beyond scientific arenas. He was a proponent of self-reliance and indigenisation in technology, which resonated with the national ethos of building a self-sustaining India. He was also involved in various initiatives outside his primary fields, including supporting population control measures, indicating his broader concerns for India's future.

His death, surrounded by both personal and professional challenges, was a significant loss to the nation. The wide range of tributes and the public grief that followed his passing reflected the deep impact he had on various spheres of Indian society. The naming of a moon crater after him by the International Astronomical Union stands as an international recognition of his contributions to science.

Vikram Sarabhai's legacy is a testament to the power of vision, dedication, and the pursuit of knowledge for the betterment of humanity. His life and work continue to inspire future generations of scientists and leaders, both in India and around the world.

❑